NIKAU'S ESCAPE

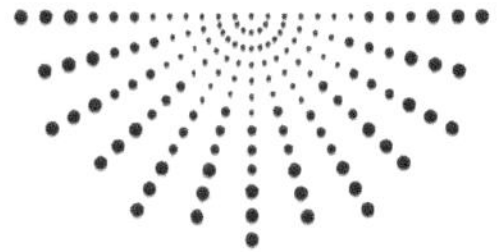

KATE S RICHARDS

GREEN ROOM HOUSE

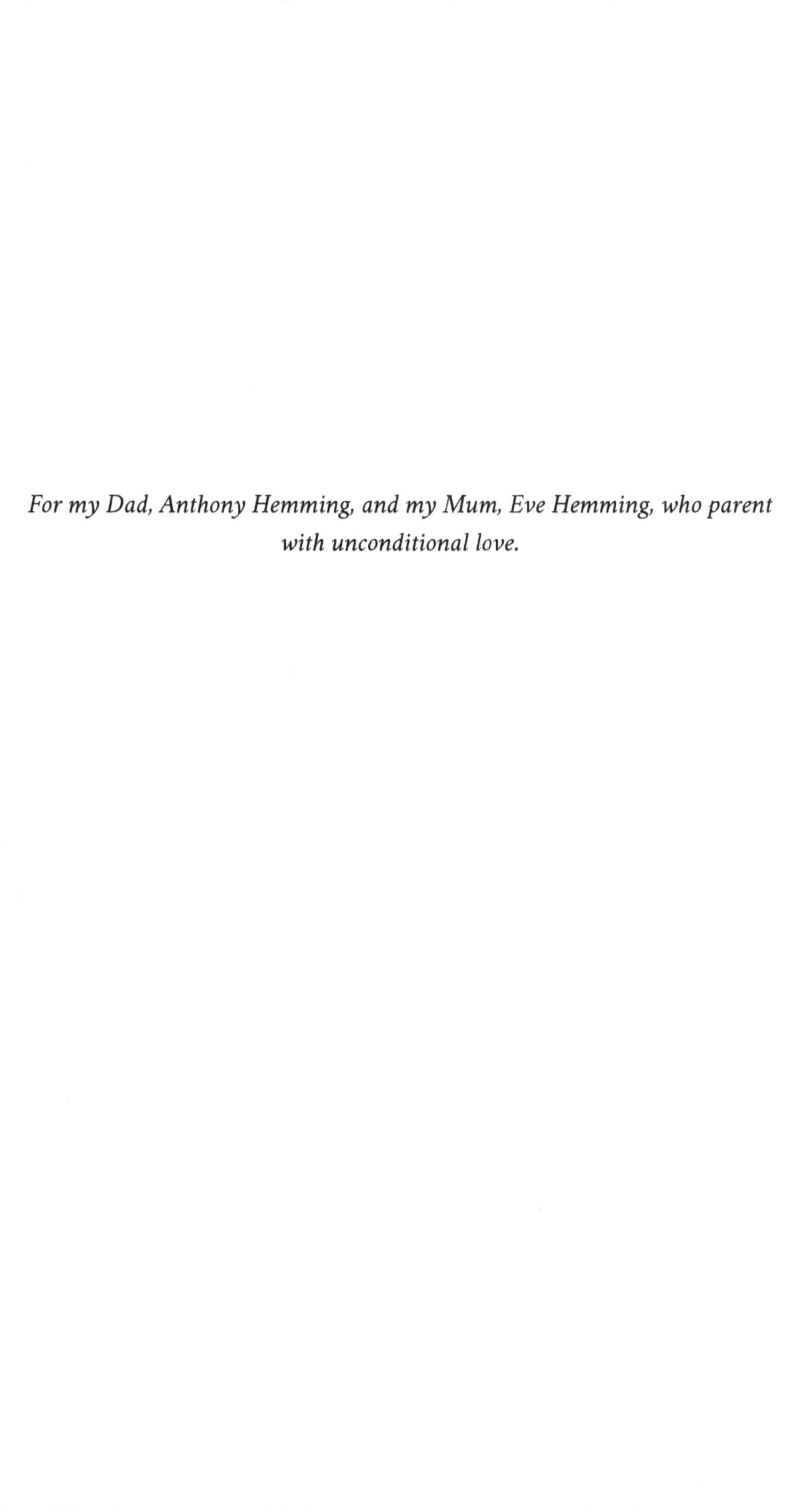

For my Dad, Anthony Hemming, and my Mum, Eve Hemming, who parent with unconditional love.

GLOSSARY

Italicised words that may require definition are listed here.

Author's note: I have placed the glossary at the front, to draw readers' attention to it as a tool.

Aotearoa: Aotearoa is the Māori name for New Zealand. It was originally used by the Māori people in reference to only the North Island but, since the late 19th century, the word has come to refer to the country as a whole. Several meanings have been proposed for the name; the most popular meaning usually given is "long white cloud", or variations thereof. This refers to the cloud formations which helped early Polynesian navigators find the country. (en.wikipedia.org)

Aroha nui: Much love, with deep affection - often used in signing off letters to friends. (https://maoridictionary.co.nz)

Bhuti: 'Brother': a polite title and term of address or reference used, especially among speakers of Sintu (Bantu) languages, when speaking to a man. (DSAE - Dictionary of South African English)

Braai: Noun 1. Short for braaivleis. Verb 1. grill (meat) over an open fire. (Dictionary)

Boerewors: A type of sausage which originated in South Africa, is an important part of South African cuisine and is popular across Southern Africa. The name is derived from the Afrikaans/Dutch words boer "farmer" and wors "sausage". (en.wikipedia.org)

Eish: South Africa. an exclamation expressive of surprise, agreement, disapproval, etc. (www.collinsdictionary.com)

Haast eagle: The Haast's eagle is an extinct species of eagle that once lived in the South Island of New Zealand, commonly accepted to be the pouakai of Maori legend. The species was the largest eagle known to have existed. (en.wikipedia.org)

Haibo wena: Is South African slang for disbelief or surprise.

Hamba kahle: "goodbye" (literally, "go well") (Wikipedia)

Hīnaki: The hīnaki (eel pot) was a basket-like pot that was set in open water with bait, or used at pā tuna (weirs). Intricately woven, the best-made hīnaki were works of art.

Ordinary hīnaki (called hīnaki tukutuku) had one entrance. When they were set without a weir, the entrance faced downstream. The eels would smell the bait, and swim upstream to find it. The hīnaki was anchored with stones and tied to a stake, a tree, or a pole driven into the stream bed. (https://teara.govt.nz/en/te-hopu-tuna-eeling/page-3)

Iwi: Iwi are the largest social units in Aotearoa Māori society. The Māori-language word iwi means "people" or "nation", and is often translated as "tribe", or "a confederation of tribes". The word is both singular and plural in the Māori language. Māori use the word rohe to describe the territory or boundaries of iwi. (en.wikipedia.org)

Kai: (noun) food, meal. (https://maoridictionary.co.nz)

Ka kite anō au i a koe:
I'll see you again. - only used when speaking to one person. For two people use kōrua instead of koe, and for three or more people use koutou instead of koe. Often shortened, incorrectly, to **Ka kite** anō or **Ka kite**. (https://maoridictionary.co.nz)

Kawakawa: (noun) kawakawa, pepper tree, *Macropiper excelsum* - a small, densely-branched tree with heart-shaped leaves. (https://maoridictionary.co.nz)

Kererū: (noun) New Zealand pigeon, kererū, *Hemiphaga novaesee-landiae* - a large green, copper and white native bush pigeon which was eaten by Māori. Kererū were one of two foods harvested during the Māori new year. (https://maoridictionary.co.nz)

Koha: (noun) gift, present, offering, donation, contribution - especially one maintaining social relationships and has connotations of reciprocity. (See more on koha here: https://maoridictionary.co.nz)

Leis: In Polynesian cultures, a lei is something that is created by someone and given to another with the intent to decorate that person for an emotional reason—usually as a sign of affection. Common reasons include greeting, farewell, affection or love, friendship, appreciation, congratulation, recognition, or to otherwise draw attention to the recipient. In Samoa, similar garlands fashioned of entire flowers, buds, seeds, nuts, plant fibers, leaves, ferns, seashells, or flower petals are called "asoa" or "ula",[8] while single flowers or clusters worn in the hair or on the ear are called sei. (en.wikipedia.org)

A lolly lei is a lei created with lollies (sweets/candy)- author's note

Mana: (noun) prestige, authority, control, power, influence, status, spiritual power, charisma (See more on mana here: https://maoridictionary.co.nz)

Maunga: (noun) mountain, mount, peak. (https://maoridictionary.co.nz)

Melktert: Melktert is a South African dessert consisting of a sweet pastry crust containing a custard filling made from milk, flour, sugar and eggs. The ratio of milk to eggs is higher than in a traditional Portuguese custard tart or Chinese egg tart, resulting in a lighter texture and a stronger milk flavour.

(en.wikipedia.org)

Melktert recipe: https://www.allrecipes.com/recipe/80160/south-african-melktert-milk-tart/

Mingimingi: (noun) broad-leaved mingimingi, Leucopogon fasciculatus, Coprosma propinqua var. propinqua and prickly mingimingi, Leptecophylla juniperina subsp. juniperina - native shrubs with small, narrow leaves which alternate or are in tufts, prickly to touch. Fruit is red, pink, blue or white and the bark is black. (https://maoridictionary.co.nz)

Miro: (noun) miro, brown pine, Prumnopitys ferruginea - a coniferous tree of lowland forest, with curved leaves arranged in two rows.

Pinkish-purple berries are eaten by kererū. (https://maoridictionary.co.nz)

Moa: (modifier) moa - large extinct flightless birds of nine subspecies. (https://maoridictionary.co.nz)

Pani popo: Pani popo are sweet coconut buns native to Samoan cuisine. Pani means "buns," and popo means "coconut." The buns themselves are made from a sweet bread dough. A separate coconut sauce is then prepared and poured over the dough before the entire dish is baked. (https://www.wikihow.com/Make-Pani-Popo)

Panikeke: Fried dough balls (recipe and blogpost here: http://www.samoafood.com/2010/11/panikeke-lapotopoto-round-pancakes.html)

Pepeha: (noun) tribal saying, tribal motto, proverb (especially about a tribe), set form of words, formulaic expression, saying of the ancestors, figure of speech, motto, slogan - set sayings known for their economy of words and metaphor and encapsulating many Māori values and human characteristics. (https://maoridictionary.co.nz)

Pikorua: A pounamu (greenstone) twist: "The Māori single twist symbol consists of a closed loop with three knots. Pikorua, as the Māori name this symbol, refers to eternal emerging paths in life. The eight-shaped single twist symbolizes the strength of the bond between two people, their loyalty and friendship." (https://www.tewahipounamu.nz/meanings/)

Piwakawaka: The New Zealand fantail is a small insectivorous bird, the only species of fantail in New Zealand. It has four subspecies: R. f. fuliginosa in the South Island, R. f. placabilis in the North Island, R. f.

penita in the Chatham Islands, and the now-extinct R. f. cervina formerly on Lord Howe Island. (en.wikipedia.org)

Pohutukawa: Metrosideros excelsa, with common names pōhutukawa, New Zealand pohutukawa, New Zealand Christmas tree, New Zealand Christmas bush, and iron tree, is a coastal evergreen tree in the myrtle family, Myrtaceae, that produces a brilliant display of red flowers made up of a mass of stamens. (en.wikipedia.org)

Pounamu (or "**greenstone**" in New Zealand English) are several types of hard and durable stone found in southern New Zealand. They are highly valued by the Māori, and hardstone carvings made from pounamu play an important role in Māori culture. Geologically, pounamu are usually nephrite jade, bowenite, or serpentinite, but the Māori classify pounamu by colour and appearance. (en.wikipedia.org)

Ricer: Derogatory urban slang for a person who makes unnecessary additions to their car to make it look and sound faster.

Rimu: Dacrydium cupressinum, commonly known as rimu, is a large evergreen coniferous tree endemic to the forests of New Zealand. It is a member of the southern conifer group, the podocarps. The former name "red pine" has fallen out of common use. (en.wikipedia.org)

Sally: Kiwi slang for Salvation Army opportunity shop.

Takkies: South African slang for trainers/sneakers.

Tamariki: (noun) children - normally used only in the plural. (en.wikipedia.org)

Tangata whenua: In New Zealand, tangata whenua is a Māori term that literally means "people of the land". It can refer to either a specific group of people with historical claims to a district, or more broadly the Māori people as a whole. (en.wikipedia.org)

Tangata tiriti: "People of the Treaty", or New Zealanders of non-Māori origin. Originally, Europeans who have a right to live New Zealand under the Treaty of Waitangi but now including peoples of other ethnic origins who live in New Zealand. (Wiktionary)

Te Ao Māori: The Māori world view (te ao Māori) acknowledges the interconnectedness and interrelationship of all living & non-living things. (https://ourlandandwater.nz/about-us/te-ao-maori)

Tokoloshe: In Zulu mythology, Tikoloshe, Tokoloshe or Hili is a dwarf-like water sprite . It is considered a mischievous and evil spirit that can become invisible by drinking water. (en.wikipedia.org)

Tōtara: Podocarpus totara is a species of podocarp tree endemic to New Zealand. It grows throughout the North Island and northeastern South Island in lowland, montane and lower subalpine forest at elevations of up to 600 m. Tōtara is commonly found in lowland areas where the soil is fertile and well drained.

Toki: The Toki had much meaning to the Māori, fashioned from stone or greenstone it was an essential tool for survival and day to day life of a Māori tribe. That's the reason the maori attribute the spiritual meaning of strength and power to the Toki, this symbol resembles determination, control, strength focus and honour. Its shape represents an axe head.

(https://wwww.tewahipounamu.nz/meanings/)

Toetoe: Austroderia is a genus of five species of tall grasses native to New Zealand, commonly known as toetoe. The species are A. toetoe, A. fulvida, A. splendens, A. richardii and A. turbaria. (en.wikipedia.org)

Tūwharetoa Iwi: Ngāti Tūwharetoa is an iwi descended from Ngātoro-i-rangi, the priest who navigated the Arawa canoe to New Zealand. The Tūwharetoa region extends from Te Awa o te Atua at Matata across the central plateau of the North Island to the lands around Mount Tongariro and Lake Taupō. (en.wikipedia.org)

For more information: http://www.Tūwharetoa.iwi.nz

Tui: The tui is an endemic passerine bird of New Zealand, and the only species in the genus Prosthemadera. It is one of the largest species in the diverse Australasian honeyeater family Meliphagidae, and one of two living species of that family found in New Zealand, the other being the New Zealand bellbird. (en.wikipedia.org)

Ureure: (noun) fruit of the kiekie, *Freycinetia baueriana* ssp. *banksii*. See also tēure, kiekie, tāwhara

(https://maoridictionary.co.nz)

Waka: Waka are Māori watercraft, usually canoes ranging in size from small, unornamented canoes used for fishing and river travel, to large, decorated war canoes up to 40 metres long. (en.wikipedia.org)

The first settlers arrived in Aotearoa (New Zealand) in large **waka** from Polynesia. (https://teara.govt.nz/en/waka-canoes)

Whakapapa: (noun) genealogy, genealogical table, lineage, descent - reciting *whakapapa* was, and is, an important skill and reflected the importance of genealogies in Māori society in terms of leadership, land and fishing rights, kinship and status. It is central to all Māori institutions. (https://maoridictionary.co.nz)

Whanau: (noun) extended family, family group, a familiar term of address to a number of people - the primary economic unit of traditional Māori society. In the modern context the term is sometimes used to include friends who may not have any kinship ties to other members. (https://maoridictionary.co.nz)

Wētā: (noun) wētā - large insects of various species found in trees and caves. There are five broad groups of wētā: tree wētā (*pūtangatanga*), ground wētā, cave wētā (*tokoriro*), giant wētā (*wētā punga*) and tusked wētā. They are active at night and all Aotearoa/New Zealand species are wingless. The females have a long, egg-laying spike at the back.

Yebo: Yes in Zulu

NIKAU'S PEPEHA

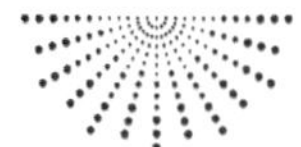

Ko Tongariro te maunga
     Ko Taupō te moana
Ko Tūwharetoa te iwi
Ko Te Heuheu te tangata
I am Nikau!

Tongariro is the mountain
     Taupō is the great inland sea
     Tūwharetoa are the people
     Te Heuheu is the man
     I am Nikau!

2

TROUBLE AT SCHOOL

NIKAU

AUCKLAND, NEW ZEALAND, 1995

The day after his father walked out of prison was the best and the worst in a series of grey days, all stacked up in an outsider's life. Nikau's morning was regular crazy. Pania hogged the bathroom. Ma slept in as usual. The juice carton was almost empty, and the cereal, stale. Nikau hunted for a pair of school socks, while Pania grumbled from the front door that she didn't want to miss the bus.

"You should get your clothes organised the night before," she nagged.

"Ma!" he yelled, but she refused to rouse herself. Nikau couldn't remember a time when she wasn't depressed.

"That's it, I'm going," said Pania, slamming the front door. Nikau extricated a pair of not overly smelly socks from under his bed. Nobody would notice. Shoes and socks on, he grabbed his rucksack and gulped down half a glass of juice.

"You need to up your game boy," said Papa Joe, looming over him as he was trying to leave.

2

Bad timing, thought Nikau.

"I had a letter from your teacher. Truancy, bad attitude, distracting others in your class, disrespectful." He counted on his fingers as he listed Nikau's faults. "I have a good mind to put you in boarding school, son."

Nikau grunted. He wished the man would stop calling him 'son'. He had a Dad, and one day he would get to know him. Then everything would be different. Better. As he meandered out the front door, the bus pulled off with Pania on it. She shook her head at him from the window. Nikau knew he should run to avoid being late. To dodge another detention. But he couldn't be bothered. He was bleary-eyed after playing Donkey Kong on his game console late into the night. He sauntered down the sidewalk instead, enjoying his regular daydream about his Dad.

One day the prison would release his father. He would arrive at school unannounced. He might pick up Nikau in a cool car; a mean muscle car, like a Mustang. They would drive down to the beach and throw a rugby ball or do whatever fathers and sons did. Maybe his Dad would tell him how rough it was in prison. He might say that he had missed his one and only son. Nikau had many stories to tell his Dad too. Like the day he forgot the words of the Kapa Haka and ended up miming and looking like a muppet on stage.

It was all Ma and Papa Joe's fault that his Dad had gone off and become a druggie and ended up in prison. He didn't want to revisit the day it all turned to custard, so he went back to creative daydreaming. He thought about all the moments of his life that his Dad had missed. Ten years of stolen moments. His first try. His first tackle. The moment he realised he was slow and couldn't keep his position as a back. He'd had nobody to share in his disappointment. Nikau had despised the sweat and blood in the ruck and rolling around in the mud. Inside, he felt weak but tried to hide it. The other boys all had proud fathers shouting them on from the sidelines. A real Dad would have talked him into overcoming his weaknesses. Told him to toughen up. Papa Joe was too busy to be at his sporting matches. As a loyal Samoan church member, he spent too much time helping random strangers, in Nikau's opinion.

Nikau had stopped going to practice and hung out with his homies instead. First, they smoked cigarettes after school and then weed. Some of the fellas had tried a few other drugs. Things got out of hand for a while. His cousin had caused a car accident, hooning around after a party. Then there was the drug-induced suicide of his classmate, Lennie. He tried to obliterate that from memory, but it clawed at him. He wasn't like those fellas. He had it under control.

Nikau gazed up from his shoelaces as a mother duck sauntered across the road, followed by seven ducklings. They couldn't have been more than a few days old. A car sped down the road towards them. Nikau jumped into the street and shooed the ducks to the sidewalk while waving at the car to slow down. A woman grinned at him as she slowed her hockey-mum SUV. They waited as the ducklings waddled by. Life as usual in *Aotearoa*. She waved and he flicked his eyebrows at her, the trace of a smile reaching the corners of his sulky mouth.

Nikau's thoughts drifted to Pania and her wilderness trips. Pania never ceased in her efforts to make him come clean. He was her pet project. Failing ongoing persuasion, she had ratted on him, and now Papa Joe expected him to go on her crazy "wilderness adventures". She even had a name for them and did fundraising and stuff. Aotearoa Ora Adventures. If he was honest, the trips were pretty epic, and snowboarding was way sicker than rugby. But this year she had got his goat. It was time to break out and be his own man, he decided. The kind of man that his real Dad would be proud of. Someone who makes their own decisions.

As he strolled along, Nikau noticed a beat-up old car crawling towards him, waking him from his daydream. It was a 1980's Japanese sedan, faded black and souped-up with a big spoiler, fenders and cheap rims. *Ricer*, he thought with a sarcastic smile. The man in the car was staring right into him, and then, after gliding by, the vehicle made a U-turn and pulled up beside him.

"Hop in, sonny," said the man.

"As if! I don't ride with strangers," said Nikau, quickening his pace.

The man laughed. "I'm no stranger. I'm your Dad," he said, pulling over into a parking space.

Two hours later, Nikau sat in the school foyer, waiting for his punishment. Time seemed to meander along, then speed up. He looked at the clock, before floating into a memory about meeting his Dad earlier that day. It seemed as if he was awash in his thoughts for hours, but when he looked back at the clock, a minute had passed. The next time his eyes wandered over to the minute hand, half an hour had gone by in a flash.

"Weird," he said aloud and laughed. Then he remembered why he was there, and his heart sped up. *What if they suspend me?* He felt a growing sense of paranoia and his legs began to shake up and down as if they had a life of their own. *They'd better not tell Papa Joe, or Ma*, he thought.

Footsteps approached down the hall. He glanced over his right shoulder to see Papa Joe, a towering hulk of a man in a white sarong and sandals, holding hands with Ma. Miss Doherty, the Deputy Principal, accompanied them. The DP's spine was as straight as an ironing board, in contrast to Ma's deflated posture. They all glowered at him. The Deputy knocked on the Principal's closed door. "Come in," said the stout woman, shaking hands with Ma and Papa Joe. She gestured for them to sit around a meeting table. Nikau became fixated by a colourful picture on the wall. In it a *kererū* soared above a pohutukawa tree, framing an aqua bay. He smiled at nothing in particular and began to hum a tune.

"Totally off his head," said the DP to the Principal.

"Yes, it appears so. We'll get the results of the urine test back later, but that will certainly confirm what we know." She turned to Ma and Papa Joe. "It's good to see you both, Mr. and Mrs..."

"Fa'aloua," said Papa Joe.

"I hope you're keeping well. But it's regrettable to have to call you in under these ... delicate circumstances. As you can see, Nikau has taken some form of narcotic. He arrived at school under the influence of drugs this morning. What was he like when he left home?"

"Nikau!" yelled Ma, "What you doing, boy? You promised you'd never do that again. Where did you get that stuff from?"

Nikau shrugged. There was no way he was going to snitch. He kept staring at the painting, wishing he was on a beach somewhere, without a worry. Time seemed to warp, stretching and skipping beats. Everyone rebuked, threatened, and even spoke gently. They didn't seem to know which approach to take with him. Ma began to blubber, but the Deputy disregarded her. The Principal offered Ma a tissue, then continued.

"Nikau needs to stay out of trouble during the holidays," she said, in a clipped voice. "If there are any reports of misbehaviour over the break, the consequences will be even more serious. We need to know that he is turning his life around. As it is, we will suspend him from school for the first week after the break." The Principal turned to face Nikau and locked her eyes with his. He couldn't look away, as much as he wanted to. Her tiny pupils looked like pinpricks in her amber irises. He felt like a worm under a microscope.

"Any further incidents and we will have to consider expulsion," said the Principal. She ran stubby fingers through a white buzz cut. "Go home now and sleep this off. Tomorrow you need to come in and see our counsellor. Understood?"

"Yes, Miss," he said, forgetting the Principal was a Mrs. Ma elbowed him in the ribs.

"Yes, Mrs McDonald."

The car trip home was torture. Ma cried and scolded him, while Papa Joe remained stony quiet at the wheel. Later, Pania looked dejected at dinner, as if she had somehow failed. Then Ma went quiet. That was the worst kind of discomfort. "You've got two choices," said Papa Joe finally. "You go with Pania and me on the trip to Ruapehu this holiday. Spend time in the outdoors. No alcohol, or any other substances. It'll be a chance to turn your life around. See if you can start to make good, clean choices."

"Or?" grunted Nikau.

"Or you stay home with Ma and paint the outside of the house and clean the windows. Do some weeding. There's a heap to do. No visits from friends though, and you'd be grounded," he said, folding his muscular arms.

Nikau thought about the house party at Piha. It was going to be a monster. Perhaps he could sneak out.

"And there'll be NO sneaking out," added Papa Joe. Ma will be checking your bed during the night, and I'll have your house key thank-you."

3

THE TOBACCO TIN

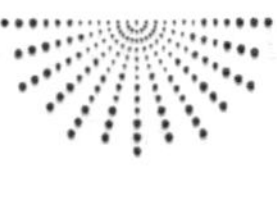

NIKAU

Papa Joe was shouting at the telly. A Tongan left-wing did a swift-footed goose-step past one Samoan defender, then another, to score the winning try. Nikau was in the kitchen wondering whether Ma would rouse herself from her book to cook tea, or if he should make two-minute noodles to fill the gap. That's when he heard a strangulated cry from the couch. It followed shortly after "Tackle him!" He heard a muffled grunt like the noise someone makes when they are in too much pain to call for help. Nikau put down the noodles and peered over the kitchen bench at Papa Joe, who was clutching his chest.

"You alright?"

Papa Joe shook his head, his round eyes pleading for help.

"Ma! Papa Joe is having a heart attack!" yelled Nikau. *What is the number you're meant to call again?* "Ma!"

Pania and Ma appeared in a flash, leaning over Papa Joe, asking him questions. Nikau stared at them, numb.

"Should I call an ambulance?" he stammered. At that, Pania grabbed the phone and dialled.

8

Nikau was still wondering to himself if the number was 911. Or was that America? *It's 111 here, isn't it?*

Fifteen minutes later, an ambulance arrived, and the paramedics stretchered Papa Joe out. Ma sat on the couch, staring into space. Pania grabbed her bag and Ma's car keys.

"Come, Ma, let's get to the hospital," she said, "I'll drive."

"Thanks, my girl," said Ma numbly.

"You coming, Nikau?" Pania asked.

Nikau looked at his bag of unopened noodles. "Na, I'll stay here and eat my tea." As he said it, he realised it sounded as if he cared more about his noodles than his stepdad.

"Sometimes I wonder if you're gonna turn out like your father," Pania muttered, "So heartless." Nikau caught her wounded expression as she charged out.

"I'll make something for you guys to eat when you get home," he called out after her.

"That'll be nice, boy," said Ma as she shuffled out behind Pania.

Nikau felt numb. He had always clashed with Papa Joe. His difficulties with his stepfather all began the day his Dad had left. The memory played over in his mind as he boiled the jug.

Papa Joe was in the kitchen, bending over Ma and Pania in a protective hug. They were crying.

"Get out!" Papa Joe thundered to Axel. His rumbling voice made the floorboards vibrate. Nikau had entered the room through an open ranch-slider and watched the scene unfold with toddler's eyes. Too young to make

sense of it, but old enough to remember. A yellow digger hung limply from his muddy hand as he observed the scene.

Axel glared at Ma and Pania. Then he stormed over to Nikau and swooped him up, charging to the front door.

"Put him down else I'll call the cops!" Ma yelled.

Like a wounded dog, Nikau's Dad placed him down, scowling.

"Never trust that man," he whispered to Nikau. "I'll be back soon, son."

Then he skulked out the doorway, without even looking over his shoulder.

Axel, his Dad, never came back. When Nikau asked Ma about his father, she had said they were getting divorced. She was silent on the details.

Once or twice, Pania called Axel a "rotten no-good" or a "loser", but Ma would shoot her a wide-eyed signal. Pania's mouth would snap shut as swiftly as a chameleon gobbling a fly. Nikau recalled a time her face went red after Ma had hushed her. His sister had folded her arms and refused to speak for the rest of dinner. Like she was a pressure cooker, holding it all in.

The jug shrilly announced boiling water for his noodles. Instead, he decided to cook up a pasta-bake for them all. They would need a feed later when they came back from the hospital. Would Papa Joe come home? Nikau felt guilty for not feeling more concerned. He firmly believed that Papa Joe and Ma were initially having a love affair, causing his Dad to leave that day. Reluctant to ask questions, he had pieced fragmented memories together into a narrative. In his version of the story, Papa Joe was guilty of stealing Ma from his Dad. Still, the colossal man had always been firm yet kind with Nikau, despite the boy's determination to never let him in.

Nikau stared out the window at a drab scene. A low cloud shrouded the city in a muted grey that sapped all the colour from life.

A faded black car across the street, blended in with the tar road, the concrete sidewalk and leafless trees. It was souped-up like a ricer's car: a too big spoiler, fenders and cheap rims.

Wait up! It's Dad! Nikau bolted to the front door, throwing it open. He was about to run across the road, but the car drove off. He had no time to see the driver.

Ten minutes later, as he was draining the pasta, the phone rang.

"Hello?" he answered, expecting Ma.

"Son, it's your Dad," said Axel.

"Oh, uh, hi."

"I need you to do something for me, my boy. It's important" he said.

"Sure, Dad, what is it?"

"Listen well, okay."

"Ah yeah."

"I have a wad of cash buried in a tin in the back yard. I saved it up for a rainy day. It's not easy to find a job when you've got a criminal record, ya know."

"Yeah, sucks," said Nikau.

"I need you to dig it up for me, mate."

"Can't you come over and dig it up yourself? No-one is home."

"Na, can't," said his Dad, not elaborating. "Remember that tree out the back yard, boy? I used to push you on the swing that hung from the thickest branch?"

"Yeah, that was choice!" said Nikau, smiling.

"Well, I need you to go to that tree and stand directly under that branch. From the trunk, walk three full strides towards the fence. Then dig. When you find the tin box, don't open it."

"Wait. What?"

"I know I can trust you, son, you've always been a top fella. On my side, ya know. Everyone needs someone like that, eh? Someone they can trust."

"Too right," said Nikau, feeling needed. "What do I do with the tin?"

"Turn left out the front door. Walk a block down the road to the T-junction. I'll be parked there, waiting for you. I'll have some takeout."

4

DIVIDED LOYALTY

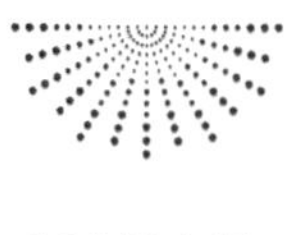

NIKAU

Nikau wrestled with an uneasy feeling, as he scavenged for a shovel in Papa Joe's tool shed. It felt wrong, going through the systematised garden implements. There were no spiderwebs in this shed, nor clutter. Everything had a place that made perfect sense, from the tools in the toolbox to the neatly hung painting of Papa Joe's childhood home. Nikau ignored his scratchy conscience, and walked over to the tree, spade in hand, focusing instead on a memory.

Dad pushed him on the swing, higher and higher until he felt he might take off beyond the blue sky, through the puffy white clouds and to the moon. He chuckled to himself, his deep voice so different from the giggling sound of the toddler in his mind. *Dad was behind him, recklessly pushing him to go beyond his comfort zone. It was exhilarating.* Dad was exciting, not like Papa Joe.

At the tree, the swing long gone, Nikau leaned against the trunk. Then he paced one, two and *ah stink!* A flower bed full of agapanthus of all things, rounded-off the corner of their yard, about where his third pace would have landed.

Nikau dug, becoming more reluctant with every thud of the shovel on clay. Dad hadn't visited all these years, hadn't contacted him, and now here he was doing the skivvy work. Shouldn't he be making a cheesy pasta for the *whanau* instead of this? But it was his Dad's rainy day fund. Dad wouldn't have asked if he didn't need the money. A *piwakawaka* flitted a fanned tail at Nikau and continued to dive-bomb him as he dug, as if in a warning.

It took half an hour of gruelling digging before he managed to slice underneath a clump of roots and topple the plant over sideways. It clung to the ground by a few stubborn tentacles. Finally, his shovel hit something hard that sent a shock into his shoulder. He collected a trowel from the shed and dug around the solid object. Then, gripping his fingers around the edges, he pulled a tin tobacco box from its clay bed.

He took it to the bathroom and washed off the clay, making a muddy mess in the basin. The tin was a rusty orange, with the words "Rugby Toasted Cigarette Tobacco" and an image of a plant and a New Zealand fern. He wondered what treasures it held. He ran his fingers along the lid and pulled upwards to see if it would give. Then the phone rang. He jerked in fright, dropping the tin on the tiled floor.

Nikau ran to the phone, answering breathlessly.

"He had a heart attack," said Pania.

"Will he be okay?" asked Nikau.

"I don't know. He's in ICU. We're going to hang here for a while."

"How bad was it?" asked Nikau.

"We're waiting to hear from the doctor. Please pray for him," said Pania, beginning to cry.

"Uh, okay. When will you be home?"

"I just said we'll be here for a while," she snapped. "I really don't know. Do you want to catch a taxi here?"

"Na, I'll finish the pasta I'm making for you guys."

"Don't worry, we'll get something from the cafeteria," said Pania with a sigh. Nikau detected disappointment in her voice. He knew she hoped he would care more.

"He'll be good as gold soon," said Nikau. "*Ka kite.*"

He hoped he would have enough time to deliver the tin and replant the agapanthus. He also needed to replace the shovel and trowel in the shed and clean the mess in the bathroom. Then a fearful dread rose up in his throat. What if Papa Joe died, the night he was digging up a tin in his stepfather's yard and sneaking around like a traitor? He startled as the phone rang again.

"You got it, son?" asked Axel in a low voice.

Immediately his feelings of guilt were overridden. It was his Dad's money, not Joe's. Dad needed him, and he was doing the right thing. He was doing what a son should do for his father. *Blood runs thicker than water*, he thought. It was a cliche, but a good one.

"Yep, I'll see you in ten."

Night had fallen, and Nikau strode out into the dimly lit sidewalk, clutching the tobacco tin. He fiddled with the lid, loosening it. It felt ready to pop open, and he decided to have a squiz. He leaned against a street lamp and pried the tin open. A healthy wad of cash met his eye. Underneath the money, he noticed the corner of something semi-translucent. Slipping his fingers underneath the notes, he pulled out a sizeable vacuum pack bag. It was swollen with colourful tablets that resembled hard sugar-shell candy, engraved with tiny letters. Nikau pulled his fingers out of the tin as if he had been stung by a scorpion. He stood under the streetlamp in front of his house, looking left and right. His hands trembled as he clutched the tin. He realised that if he delivered the ziplock bag to his Dad, his father might end up in jail again before he even had a chance to get to know him. *I can't let you do that*, he thought.

There was enough money in the tin to tide Axel over until he found a job. Without thinking twice, Nikau lifted the plastic lid of their rubbish bin and dropped the stash into it. He covered it with an empty chip packet and lowered the bin top. It felt like an irreversible choice.

Nikau's heart pounded as he walked down the street with a less weighty tin. He hoped his Dad wouldn't open it until later. Next time they were together he would find a way to explain. This was their season to be a father and son, and he didn't want his Dad ruining it by getting caught dealing. He suspected the pills to be meth. Nikau swallowed hard, remembering Lennie's decline. It was no good that stuff. No good.

He hoped the rubbish collectors wouldn't discover it. Then Ma might have to answer some curvy questions. He shelved that worry for later. For now, though, it was likely his Dad was getting impatient. Nikau picked up his pace.

A car rolled past as Nikau cradled the tin of cash, his hoodie pulled over his face, feeling like a fugitive. At the sight of the car, his mood lifted. He had worked up a gnawing hunger, and his thoughts soon turned to the takeout his Dad had promised him. He was so hungry he could have scoffed down his share, his Dad's share and the pasta dish he still needed to bake.

Nikau flung the side door open and slipped inside the black car, careful not to sit on a spring that bust through the upholstery. A toy mustang hung from the rearview mirror. The vehicle smelled of nicotine.

Axel snatched the box from him.

"Chur, that's beaut cuzzie," he said.

Nikau laughed.

"Dad, you're not Māori… and anyway, that's not how we speak,"

Axel looked offended. "Well, you're part Māori, like your Ma. I was only trying to…"

"Be yourself, Dad. It's cool."

"Okay. Sweet. How did it go?"

"A fair bit of elbow grease. Now, where's the *kai*? I'm so hungus I could eat a whole horse!"

Axel looked uncomfortable.

"Ah rats, I forgot."

"You forgot? The burgers?"

Axel nodded, his expression flippant.

Nikau felt a stab of disappointment. After years of waiting for his father to come back, the man had charged into his life, expecting skivvy work. Yet he had not even provided a feed. Thoughtless. He felt like taking back the tin. He was hungry-angry.

"I'm no good at this father-son business. It's been a while, eh? Give me time, mate."

Nikau scowled at his jandals, arms folded, fists clenched.

"Here, take this," said Axel, passing him a rolled-up joint.

"Na. I got into trouble yesterday at school after smoking with you," he said moodily. "I… I need to quit."

"What for? Doesn't it make you feel mellow?" asked Axel, smiling.

"Not anymore. It used to. Nowadays, it makes me paranoid."

"Well then, you need something a little stronger to take off the edge. I've got something in this tin…"

"Na, I'm good," said Nikau, waving the tin away.

Axel grunted.

"Dad, you need to come clean if you want to get work and stuff. Now that you're out of jail."

"Don't you be telling me…" said Axel, his pale face reddening.

"Okay, chill."

They sat in silence for a long minute. Axel was about to open the tin when Nikau asked, "Dad, were you parked outside our house earlier? I saw your car. Were you watching me?"

"Yeah, only' coz I didn't want your Ma or Joe to answer the phone.

I was waiting for them to go out before giving you your assignment, son."

"That's kinda creepy, Dad."

"Look, it's not easy to make it after the slammer. I don't have many contacts on the outside. Only Vito, and he's unreliable. You're my boy. I used to carry you over my shoulder, remember?"

Nikau felt his emotions rising. He tried not to swallow as he didn't want Axel seeing his vulnerability. He quashed his need for love and connection, biting his lower lip.

"There's so much I wanna know about you, Dad. Like why did you end up in prison? Why did you never visit us or write?"

"I haven't got time to chat now," said Axel dismissively. "I have business to attend to, but I'll catch up with ya soon, boy. Then we can have that heart to heart." Axel patted Nikau firmly on the back.

He felt empty — and had so many questions.

"When will I see ya again, Dad?" asked Nikau, hating himself for being so needy. "Maybe we can, I dunno, throw a rugby ball, or … something."

"I'll call you again soon," said Axel, softening. "I need you to help me out with a few things a'right?"

Nikau had a queasy feeling in his gut. Skivvy work again. Probably dodgy.

"I'm going away for a few days," said Nikau, suddenly relieved to be getting distance from his Dad. He needed time to process. There was a chasm between the father he had yearned for and this unfathomable character who had arrived in his life expecting favours.

"Where to?"

"We're going snowboarding at Mount Ruapehu," he said, starting to smile at the thought of it.

"Straight up, gee?"

"You're doing it again," said Nikau, shaking his head at his Dad's attempt to speak his lingo.

He wasn't sure if Axel looked sad or angry. The man's jaw clenched.

"Later, Dad," said Nikau, climbing out the car.

"See ya," said Axel.

He walked back to a cold, dark house, hungry and tired. He flicked on a few lights. Nikau devoured the cold pasta, forking it straight from the pot on the stove without any cheese. It had been a maniacal couple of hours and Nikau needed to cover up his actions in the yard and bathroom before the others got home. He set to cleaning the mess he had made. While he worked, he said a silent prayer for Papa Joe. A schism of divided loyalty sliced between Nikau's sinews and bone.

For the moment, he forgot about the ziplock bag in the rubbish bin under the streetlight. He didn't even think about what his Dad might do when he discovered it was missing.

5

PAPA JOE'S QUEST

PANIA

Papa Joe propped himself up with a pillow as Pania pulled a chair alongside him. The colour had drained from his cheeks. An antiseptic smell lingered on his skin. A drip pierced into a vein under his Pe' a tattoo. The man who was a mighty figure of strength and kindness, reduced to a frail patient in a gown. Pania shivered. Still, he held his dignity, stoic and uncomplaining.

"Don't look so worried, Pania. I didn't cark it."

"Pa!"

"I'm still here." He squeezed her hand. "My old ticker is a bit munted, though. Doc reckons I'll have to have a bypass."

Pania nodded gravely.

"It'll be a good thing," he reassured her. "Give me a new lease on life, they say."

"Ah well in that case…" she smiled.

"Now, I want to talk to you about the mountain trip…"

"Ah, don't worry Pa, I'll call it off. I need to be here for you, and Ma."

"No!" he said, sitting upright.

20

"Pa, relax. The doc said you need to stay calm."

"Okay, but listen to me, please." He wheezed.

Pania waited for him to take a few deep breaths and calm his heart rate.

"Nikau needs this," he said. "I get the feeling he's at a turning point in his life. He could go either way. You and I have put so much into AOA. Into getting it off the ground and…"

"Yeah, and when you're better, after your bypass we can…"

Papa held up his hand, his forehead creasing.

"Listen to me," he said in a thin voice.

"Sorry. I'm all ears."

"I want you to go ahead with the trip. Invite a friend with you to lend you a hand. And you've got those surfer friends to help you. You said they're good blokes, right? Take Nikau and a few of his mates and give them a time to remember."

Pania sat silent for a moment, waiting for him to continue. But he didn't. He stared out the window, lost in thought.

"Pass me some water please, princess." He sipped and cleared his throat. "I've been thinking, Nikau needs a new challenge," he said.

Pania cut in. "Āe, he does. Last year he was snowboarding from the top of Turoa, no sweat. But then he came back and carried on being a ratbag. We need to catch his attention with something epic. Like climbing to the top of the mountain and peering inside the crater!"

"I wouldn't do that. Not safe. But I agree that he needs an epiphany of sorts," said Papa Joe.

Pania thought about the moments in her life when joy had cut through like a beam of sunlight, unanticipated, and glorious. Although fleeting, those brief awakenings deepened her desire to be fully conscious. She had no interest in numbing her mind. If only Nikau could realise the wonder of being present.

"It'll take more than a regular ski trip to shake him awake," said Pania.

"Too right," said Papa Joe, scratching his chin. Then he smiled nostalgically.

"When I was a young fella," he said, "we skied the Mangaturuturu Glacier. It was indescribable. Nikau would never forget something like that," he said. His eyes focused on a remembered place and time, far outside the window.

"Where's that? How do you get there?" asked Pania.

"Well," he said, "You catch the ski lift to the top of Mount Ruapehu, on the Turoa side. In those days, mind you, we had to tramp the whole way with skins. For you guys it's easy. From the top, ski to your right. Ski across all the recreational slopes." He leaned towards Pania and made eye contact. She paid him her full attention.

"You need to keep your altitude for as long as possible, no matter how tempting the piste runs look to you. When you get past the last ski run, you'll need to use your skins to climb up to Pare Saddle."

"How will I get my bearings?"

"I'll mark it out on a map for you. When you get to the top of Pare Saddle, you'll see the sweetest ride rolled out before you. The snow is untouched, like a new tub of ice-cream, and the glacier slides down into gorges below. It's a touch of the transcendent." He paused.

"The forest is in the distance, but don't go that far. Stop at a thousand feet, and then climb back up. That's the character-building part of the exercise," he said chuckling. Then Papa Joe began to cough.

"Pa, no more stories, okay. I've got a mental picture of it. I'll make sure I bring in a map for you to mark out for me. But now you need to rest."

"You're so bossy," he said tiredly. "But promise me that you'll try. For Nikau."

"Okay, Pa, I'll do my best — as long as you promise to rest and get better."

"I'll be a box of birds before you know it," he said. Then he closed his eyes. Pania sat quietly, holding his hand and watching his chest move up and down slowly. Ma came in with a plastic cup of weak tea.

"You get home, girl, and see if Nikau needs help with dinner. I'll stay here tonight. Take the car. I don't want to pay for overnight parking. You can fetch me tomorrow."

"I'll nip home and get your toothbrush and a book first," said Pania. "And then I'll head home again. Nikau can take care of himself."

Ma raised her eyebrows sarcastically.

"Thanks, love. And please bring me a jumper. It's chilly in here."

"Sure, Ma." Pania leaned down and kissed her Ma on her soft forehead. "He's going to be good as gold soon," she said.

Ma managed a weak smile and turned to watch Papa Joe, who had fallen asleep with his mouth wide open as the medication started to take effect.

Pania's shoulders drooped as she left, carrying Papa Joe's expectations like a laden backpack. She needed to find strength to lead the Ruapehu trip. And courage to carry out Pa's suggestion of a trek to a glacier. Papa Joe was her rock, and always had been. Yet now he was frail and he needed her to step up. She made up her mind to try. For Pa, and for Nikau.

6

LAST NIGHT IN AFRICA

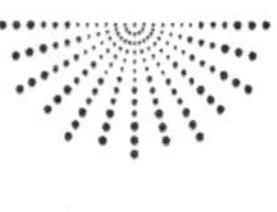

JABU

GREEN ROOM HOUSE, DURBAN, SOUTH AFRICA

Jabu felt restless. He wondered if the surf trip to New Zealand would cure him of a grating feeling that he couldn't place. Ashamed of his ingratitude, he tucked the rising agitation away with his t-shirts. The feeling was being neatly folded and placed in his travel case.

"Why so blue?" asked Alexia, wandering into his room uninvited. Not a sister in blood, but she felt like family. She glanced over his open suitcase.

"Gee, you're neat!" she said, flipping through his clothes. "But it's easy to pack when you're a guy, right." She pouted for effect, showing off her new fuschia lipstick. She wore her favourite colours, a pink t-shirt and a turquoise beach skirt that complemented her mahogany complexion. She had broad shoulders and strong arms from surfing, yet remained feminine. Jabu remembered the wild-haired waif they had brought in from the streets. Now she was South Africa's top female junior surfer. Like a competitive sibling, he felt proud and

24

envious at the same time.

"Hey, don't be so nosey," he said, as she mussed through his things.

"You are grouchy today. I don't understand it. You're going on an epic trip. Why aren't you happy?"

Jabu wondered the same thing. He shrugged.

Kyle bounded in. *Doesn't anyone knock around here?* Jabu wondered. Casting an eye over Jabu's luggage, Kyle laughed. "You'll freeze to death in the mountains if you don't pack warm clothes, dude."

"This is Durban, in case you haven't noticed," said Alexia. "I've only ever seen Jabu in one jumper."

"*Yebo*," said Jabu. "I only own one jumper and a pair of jeans."

Kyle pulled Jabu's well-worn jumper from his wardrobe and lobbed it at him. "No stress, I'll take you shopping when we're in Auckland. We'll pick up a ski jacket and gear."

"What does he need that for?" asked Alexia, looking perplexed. "I thought he was going as your surf training partner."

"I'll explain later," said Jabu shortly. "Now can you two please give me some space."

Alexia and Kyle raised their eyebrows at one another and shrugged. Alexia clicked her tongue.

"*Haibo wena!*" she said, following Kyle out the door, and leaving Jabu to pack away his emotions.

Later that evening, Jabu felt unsettled again. For the first time in his years at Green Room House, he was aware of an agitated, vague pining. It was a scratchy, claustrophobic feeling, in direct contrast to the homely scene in which he sat pondering. He had finished reading the last page of Peter Pan while the children were delaying getting ready for a story. He always liked to vet a book before sharing it with them. He concluded that the tale was too brutal for these children, who had endured more than any should.

As Jabu's long brown fingers stroked the spine of the book, he reflected on the character of Peter. What was it about this impish boy that perturbed him? It was not his implied violence or impetuous bossiness that bothered Jabu. Those characteristics were disparate from his own nature, and while they made him decide that Peter Pan was not a role model for the children, he plumbed his mind for the cause of his turbulence. Deep down, he knew and recognised the answer as it rose to his conscious level of thought.

Peter, would never grow up. He chose not to. As the children gathered around him, he saw himself mirrored in this immortalised character. Jabu had rescued 'Father's' street boys and girls, and given them a home, as Peter had gathered up the Lost Boys and built them a tree home.

"Are you going to read us that story?" asked a five-year-old girl. She had only recently come to the house, hungry and skittish after months of living rough. Her big eyes gazed up at him.

"Not sure," he said, as the others began to settle on beanbags around him like feathers after a pillow fight.

When Jabu had forfeited a scholarship to a surfing school overseas, he had done so partly for them. But he acknowledged that in committing to them, he had fulfilled his deep need for family.

The day his mother had died, Jabu had never felt so alone. He still did, sometimes. Yet, every morning, he busied himself with the routine of helping ready the children for surf school. Then he coached them on the beach, and in the ocean, followed by lunch and class time with Teacher Josh in the afternoons. It was the routine that gave him comfort, the children that satisfied his need to be loved. Yet, in a painful moment of truth, he realised that unlike Peter Pan, he was ready to grow up. But he did not have a Mr and Mrs Darling to pass the children on to. So, also unlike Peter, he was not free to choose. At that moment, he despised Peter Pan for his freedom.

"You gonna read that story or must I?" asked Vusi, trying to snatch the book from his hands.

"Sorry, I was thinking," said Jabu, clutching the book tight.

"You've been daydreaming too long, *bhuti*. The kids are ready for bed," said Vusi. Jabu felt as if his role as captain was being challenged.

"No, it's okay Vusi, sit. I've got a story to tell them," Jabu asserted.

Vusi folded into a beanbag, his arms wrapped around his legs, pouting.

The children of Green Room House, no longer sleeping rough on the streets, snuggled around Jabu's bare feet. He smiled down at their sleepy faces. He had decided to tell them about his pending adventure. He was sure he could make it sound as engaging as any of Peter Pan's exploits.

"I'm flying to the land of the long white cloud," said Jabu. That got their attention. The children shuffled on their bottoms, moving in closer.

"Is it always cloudy there?" asked the youngest.

"I sure hope not," he said. "But I expect snow. We're going snowboarding." Jabu leaned in towards them. "I also heard the waves are epic."

"You get to surf and snowboard?" asked Bongani.

"*Yebo*. Kyle asked me to be his training partner, remember. He's surfing in that international tournament."

"Oh ya. Cool," said Bongani, with ill disguised envy." But how come you get to snowboard?"

Jabu wondered to himself how he had got so lucky. He explained that Kyle's friend Pania had invited them to go snowboarding, before the surf season.

"The unique thing is, we're snowboarding on a volcano!"

"A volcano!" A few children called out together.

"Yep, but it's not active at the moment," he said reassuringly.

"Is Pania Kyle's girlfriend?" asked Alexia.

"Nope. I'm not going all the way across the Pacific to tag along in a romance," said Jabu, rolling his eyes in mock annoyance.

"Alright, chill. I'm only kidding," said Alexia.

"Do they have lions and elephants?" asked an inquisitive new girl. She sat on Alexia's lap, cradling a scruffy teddy.

"No, but they have a unique flightless bird, called a Kiwi," he said, smiling.

"Do they speak Zulu in the cloudy land?" asked Sipho.

"I doubt it. I've heard they speak English and the language of the first people, the Māori people."

"It sounds like you've been studying up," said Alexia.

"I've done some reading. And Kyle has filled me in on what he's learnt from Pania."

He had piqued their curiosity, and now the questions were flying at him all at once. Jabu faced their questions with good humour. At nineteen, he was the closest to a father-figure that the children currently had.

"What's this place called?" asked Sipho.

"Well," said Jabu, "this place, the land of the long white cloud, is called Aotearoa, or New Zealand."

"I'm pretty sure that's not how you pronounce it," said Vusi.

Jabu ignored Vusi's interjection.

"Watch out for sharks and volcanoes!" piped the new girl, twirling a braid around her pinkie finger. "Pwomise you'll come home." She fought back the tears.

"I promise," said Jabu. "Now it's time for bed, okay."

The young orphans sprung up to hug or high five him before climbing into their bunks. Jabu imagined their minds slipping into sleep, with thoughts of adventures in faraway lands.

"Tonight I'm going to dream about a Kiwi on a snowboard in a land of fluffy clouds," said the littlest.

"I hope I don't dream about sharks and volcanoes," said a boy with a gravelly voice.

Jabu smiled to himself, before slipping out the dormitory to the sound of sleepy chatter. He left the door ajar, allowing a sliver of light, as they liked it.

An hour later, when Jabu was almost asleep, he heard footsteps approaching. He rubbed his eyes and looked up at Alexia, who hovered at his bedside in her pyjamas.

"What's up, Gecko?" he asked.

"I'm fourteen. Would you stop calling me that already?"

"Okay, Titanium Girl," he said chuckling.

Alexia punched his arm. "Ouch. Okay, okay. Alexia it is."

She paused, then took a deep breath before speaking.

"Please come back in time to watch me surf in the SA Junior Champs. If I win, I'll qualify to surf the internationals again."

"I'll do my best," said Jabu.

"It would mean so much to me... to have you there cheering me on," she added shyly.

Jabu nodded. "As long as we don't get entangled in another crazy adventure, I'll be there."

"No more kidnappers or great escapes!" said Alexia, turning to go. "Night then."

"Night, Gecko."

She shot him a fake glare, flung her braids over her shoulders and sauntered out.

Something about the idea of coming back to the old routine left him feeling heavy again. But he wouldn't let Alexia down. He rolled over and made a promise to himself that he would come back to support his 'adopted sis', no matter what.

Trying to sleep, he realised that something would have to change in his life. The truth was, he had outgrown his roles as House Father at Green Room House and surf instructor at Kids Surf 4 Life. But what else could a black teen do in a new South Africa that hadn't changed all that much? He only had a high school diploma, and his best surfing years were behind him.

Like King Solomon once wrote, "There is a season for every-thing..." and he would need to break out and find his new purpose. But first, he would have to hand over his captaincy to someone trust-worthy. Jabu tossed over, plumped up his pillow and sighed. He decided to unpack thoughts about his future when he returned from New Zealand. Clipping a mental case closed, he allowed his mind to turn to the excitement of the trip. He fell asleep picturing a mythical Māui, fishing the north island out of a deep blue abyss.

7

IMPRESSIONS OF AOTEAROA

JABU

PIHA, NEW ZEALAND

The sky in the land of the long white cloud was unexpectedly blue that first morning. Jabu could not see a white puff in any direction. Leaves sparkled, reflecting the spring sunlight with freshly washed intensity. Majestic forest on either side of the ridge road revealed only flashes of view. He caught a glimpse of a harbour on the left and one on the right, far below the ancient volcanic ranges. Then the towering *kauri* trees denied him any further outlook for a while.

"Look left," said Kyle after they had snaked along for many miles. Jabu glimpsed Karekare beach, wild and rugged, a dramatic way below the mountain top road. It was famous for annual beach horse races, and the moody movie, *The Piano*. A sharp rock, shaped like a shark fin, jutted out of the wild west coast sea.

He wondered whether Scenic Drive was named after the flashes of bright blue water or the emerald rainforest. The native trees were almost overwhelming in their ubiquitous green. So different from the dry African scrub he knew so well. He felt invigorated by the newness while knowing the deep love he had for his homeland was unshakable. Kyle broke into his dreamlike reverie. "This trip will be wicked. Wait until you see the beach, dude."

Jabu's surf buddy navigated the hired sedan along a windy road that cut between boulders, down a hill, before the view of Piha opened up on their left. Kyle swerved suddenly, pulling over to a lookout point. The surfers climbed out of the vehicle and stood at the cliff edge, breathing it in. Rows of inviting waves rolled into a bay, tucked between two grand rock outcrops. Like lion sentinels, the rocks guarded the surf against the Tasman Sea beyond. Lines of waves, breaking from the left, promised a perfect ride.

"It'll be cold," said Kyle, once they were standing at the water's edge, ten minutes later. Jabu thought about Durban ocean temperatures, where it was mild enough to surf in boardshorts, even in winter. A broken wave swept over his feet.

"Eish, bro! Chilly," he said, reluctantly pulling on a wetsuit, one leg at a time.

The black beach mirrored the sky above with a glossy sheen. Jabu followed Kyle across the iron-rich volcanic sand, icy waves splashing around his ankles. Once in, Jabu paddled after Kyle along a rip that sucked them out next to the left sentinel. They hit a few breakers on their way and duck-dived deftly beneath them. Out at the backline, they paddled sideways off the rip and sat on their boards. Jabu was not disappointed to meet a lull in the waves. It was a chance to get his bearings and catch his breath. The rocky outcrops loomed around them in craggy splendour.

"Hey, thanks for inviting me on this trip," said Jabu. "Place is stunning!"

"No worries," said Kyle, flicking wet blond hair out of his tanned face and grinning. "All paid for by my sponsors. And besides, you're doing me a solid. Best training partner I could wish for."

Jabu smiled. He had so many memories of surfing with Kyle, not all positive, mind. But he knew that his reckless style of surfing inspired Kyle to push the limits, and he was glad to help.

A shapely swell rose behind them.

"Race you for it," said Kyle, paddling fast.

Jabu watched him go, knowing the second wave in the set would be sweeter.

They carved and shredded, embedding themselves into the dramatic setting. Hours later, Jabu couldn't endure the chilly water a moment longer.

"I'm fixing for something to eat and a hot chocolate," he said shivering.

Kyle laughed.

"It's my African blood! said Jabu indignantly. He wondered if he would ever feel his feet again.

"Let's end on a good one," said Kyle, always after one more sweet ride. Jabu enjoyed a brief wave and paddled in. He watched from the shore as Kyle shredded like a maestro.

"Looking sharp bro," said Jabu as Kyle finally padded up the beach with his board under his arm.

Kyle smiled humbly, peeling the leash strap off his ankle and hooking his board underarm. Jabu tried not to shiver as they strolled up the beach.

"I'm looking forward to meeting your friend," said Jabu, teeth chattering.

"She'll be here today," said Kyle. "They're raising funds for one of Nikau's friends to come on the trip."

"Who's Nikau?"

"Her wayward brother. She's trying to get him straight. He's the whole reason she started Aotearoa Ora Adventures. She wanted to get him into the wilderness and off weed."

"Ah, righteous bro. Like us getting Sipho and Vusi off glue and hooked on surfing. Did it work?"

"He's a work in progress," said Kyle, furrowing his brow. "Ah, there they are!" He pointed at a long queue that led to a trestle table on the pavement at the carpark. As they got closer, Jabu could read the sign hanging from the table.

Aotearoa Ora Adventures
Sausage Sizzle Fundraiser
Gold coin

"What's a sausage sizzle, bro?"

"It's a Kiwi version of our *boerewors* roll. Quick and easy. You hungry?"

Jabu raised his eyebrows as if to say, "What do you think!"

As the queue shortened, Jabu noticed a teenage girl serving the sausages. She was tall, with glossy black hair that fell over broad shoulders. Her almond-shaped eyes turned upwards at the edges, giving her a curious expression. She wore a twisted greenstone necklace. Later he would learn that greenstone was called *pounamu* in New Zealand and that the twist design symbolised the bond between two people.

At her side was a taller, but younger looking teenage boy. He shared her honeyed complexion and aquiline nose, but while her eyes were a rich brown, his were a pale, almost translucent green. His thick brown hair curled out from under a beanie. While her full lips turned up in the corners, his mouth turned down.

"Kyle!" she said, leaning over the table to hug Jabu's friend. "You've been for a surf already, I see. And is this Jabu?" she asked, her eyes meeting his for the first time.

Jabu felt as if his legs were giving way. He wondered if it was jetlag. Or was he still feeling the motion of the waves? A girl couldn't have this effect on him. No way.

"Hi," he said.

"Onions?" she asked him.

"Uh, what?"

"Do you want onions with your sausage?" she asked.

"Oh, uh, no thanks. Tomato sauce please," he said.

"Sauce is over there," she pointed.

Jabu's face felt hot. He didn't know the sausage sizzle drill.

She rolled a sausage in a slice of bread and handed it on a napkin to Jabu. Kyle squirted his sausage sizzle with mustard and tomato sauce.

Jabu looked at him sideways, shaking his head. "You've got strange taste buds," he scoffed.

Kyle grinned.

"I'll catch up with you guys later," Pania said, turning to the next customer.

"Howzit, Nikau," said Kyle as they moved along the length of the table. Nikau flicked his eyebrows back at Kyle, in greeting.

Shortly afterwards, Jabu and Kyle sat on the beach with wetsuits peeled down to the waist and towels wrapped around their shoulders. They wolfed down the hot sausage sizzles and licked their sticky fingers clean.

"So, how did you meet Pania?" asked Jabu casually.

"I met her in the surf, here at Piha a couple of years ago," said Kyle, staring out at the breaking waves. "We were bobbing up and down on our boards like gulls on a swell and got chatting. We realised that our life purposes were similar. You see, Pania and her Papa Joe started Aotearoa Ora Adventures to get Nikau and his friends off weed. They were binge drinking, smoking weed and even dabbling in stronger drugs."

Jabu nodded, thinking of how they started Kids Surf 4 Life to get street children off glue and stoked on surfing.

Kyle went on. "Pania told me they wanted to get these kids stoked on snowboarding, or anything outdoorsy. She thought that would give them a fresh perspective."

"She sounds wise," said Jabu, interested in hearing more about her. He sipped his cola before asking, "So did Pania invite us snowboarding because we run a similar programme?"

"Yeah, pretty much. She said we could be like mentors to the young lads, especially Nikau," said Kyle. "And we can share experiences. What we've learnt, mistakes we've made. That sort of thing."

Jabu nodded again, taking it all in. Kyle had touched on the subject when they were at Green Room House.

"I'm so amped about it. How much time will we spend at the mountain?"

"About three weeks. Enough time for us to learn how to snowboard or ski. Pania reckons that being surfers, it'll be a breeze. And when we come back, we'll have a full month to train for the surfing comps."

"Perfect."

"Hey," said Pania, interrupting their chat. She sat down beside Jabu. He noticed her painted toenails as she wiggled her feet in the sand.

"Papa Joe had a heart attack," she announced in a quiet voice.

"Oh no, is he…?" Kyle began to ask.

"He's alive. It was a mild attack. But he's in hospital recovering," she replied.

"I'm sorry to hear it," said Kyle.

"Yep, it sucks."

"Doesn't he usually lead the snowboarding trips?" asked Kyle after a long silence.

"He always has — every single one. So now I'm expected to lead it, and I don't know if I can. I'm only seventeen, ya know, and Nikau and his mates are ratbags. Trouble seems to follow that brother of mine."

"Hey, we'll be there," said Jabu, surprising himself.

"Thanks." She smiled at him, and for a moment, he forgot he was cold and hungry. It was as if she clearly saw him. And that made him warm inside.

"I feel such a responsibility to make it happen," she went on. "If we don't go, Nikau and his mates will end up at a massive party, high on weed or goodness knows what else. They'd be loitering about, or hooning and getting into trouble. Papa Joe threatened to ground him, but I doubt that would stop the fella."

"Hey, we'll make it happen," said Kyle, resting his hand on her shoulder. "Don't stress."

Pania frowned. Jabu imagined that she didn't like anyone telling her what emotion to feel.

"The funny thing is, Nikau seems excited to come along suddenly. I couldn't believe it when he offered to help out with the sausage sizzle today."

Jabu thought that Pania's brother didn't seem entirely cheerful about it, but he kept his observation to himself.

"Anyone want leftovers?" boomed Nikau from the table.

Jabu had worked up an appetite in the surf.

"Yes, please!" he called back.

"Thanks," said Kyle, "and we'll help you pack away," he added.

They worked together, loading gas cylinders and cookers into Papa Joe's ute. Jabu and Kyle wolfed down sausages as they packed the leftovers into a chilly bin.

"Ew," said Nikau. "I've smelled those all day. I want to go home and eat salad!"

"Yeah right," quipped Pania.

Jabu helped Pania fold up the trestle table. They locked the cash tin and placed it with a hand-written sign in the cab.

"Do ya think we made enough for Ben and Tipene to join us?" asked Nikau.

"I hope so," said Pania, hopping into the driver's seat. "Pick you guys up on Monday," she said out the window. "Make sure you pack warmly eh."

"Yep, Kyle and I are going shopping for ski jackets tomorrow!" said Jabu.

Kyle gave him a quizzical look.

"See ya later," Pania called out as the ute pulled out of the carpark.

"Are we seeing them later tonight?" asked Jabu.

Kyle laughed heartily.

"No, dork, that's how we say 'bye', in New Zealand."

8

SERENE SUPERVOLCANO

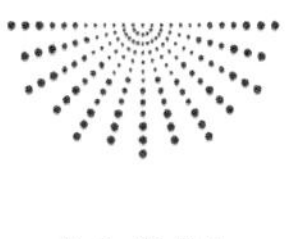

JABU

Jabu wasn't sure if he was more captivated by Aotearoa or Pania. He found it difficult to distinguish between his fascination with her and her land. Pania was a vibrant mosaic. Her melodic voice, the stories she told about the first people, and the occasional Māori words she used — pieced together in an engaging portrait. He found New Zealand relentlessly startling in its vistas — alternating between pastoral and intense. Pania, with her bubbling laughter and sun-kissed skin, was like a praise song to the land. She was often silent, like the hills, talking only when she had something of significance to share.

Pania and her friend Areta took turns to drive a full van. They were the camp leaders. Jabu and Kyle sat in the next row, appreciating the scenery. Nikau and his friends, Tipene and Ben mucked around in the back seat. Jabu leaned in towards the gap between the two cab seats to watch the view unfold ahead. He gasped as they turned a corner, revealing Lake Taupō in the foreground and distant snow-covered mountains.

"Good place for some kai," said Pania.

"Can we get takeaways?" asked Nikau from the back seat.

"Na, I've packed a picnic, Mr Moneybags," she said, eliciting exaggerated groans from the back.

Pania guided the van into a parking area at five-mile bay. A vast lake lapped the shore of a beach smothered with smooth stones. Nikau, Tipene and Ben entertained themselves by whipping each other with reeds while Jabu and Kyle skimmed stones off the glassy lake. Jabu picked up a white disk, turning it over in his hand. It had more holes than swiss cheese. It was almost as light as the air bubbles that pocked the surface.

"Dude, check this out," said Jabu, passing Kyle the pumice stone.

Pania and Areta laid food on a picnic table, under the shade of a *pohutukawa* tree. Once the sandwiches and fruit were set out on paper plates, they all sat down.

"Listen up, and I'll tell you a story," said Pania, in the tone of a seasoned orator. "Long ago a massive volcanic eruption caused this crater. It happened when Moa still roamed through the bushes and trees covered every foot of land, way before Kupe arrived on his *waka*. Geologists reckon it has erupted twenty-eight times since."

Jabu's eyes grew wide. The lake stretched out almost as far as the eye could see. If this lake was the crater, he couldn't imagine how immense the eruption would have been.

"Oh, my word! Could it blow again?" he asked.

"Well, the most recent eruption was nearly 200 years after Jesus. Around a hundred and eighty A.D. or so…" added Areta.

"Our ancestors passed on the story, that when it blew, it kicked out so much ash that the world was dark for two whole weeks," said Pania. "They passed it down from generation to generation."

Jabu gazed out at the placid blue waters. Nothing to indicate violence. Translucent ripples lapped the shore. Nikau and his friends tucked into the kai. Jabu thought they seemed untouched by the story and the beauty of the lake. He imagined it was all old news to them.

Then Nikau piped up. "My nana tells it different," he said, wiping away a crumb. "She reckons when the chief tohunga of the local iwi saw how barren the basin was, he wasn't too chuffed. He thought, 'I'd better do something about this,' So he chucked a *tōtara* tree into the crater to plant a new forest."

"Seriously bro, and then what happened?" asked Ben, who had never ventured beyond his city suburb.

"Well, the branches pierced the ground of course, and water seeped up, filling the crater."

"That's so cool," said Jabu. "And what's this?" he asked, passing Pania the pumice stone.

"That's lava. The explosion was so violent that the gases escaped quickly, creating all these bubbles."

Jabu held it in his hand. He stared out at the snowy mountains in the distance. He wondered if they too had stories, geological and mythological. And history. And science. This wasn't a land to travel through with your eyes and ears closed.

"Thank-you," he said to Pania.

"What for?"

"For being our guide," he said. Their eyes met, and Jabu looked down, clutching the pumice. He would be sure to place it back on the beach before they packed up.

"Hey Nikau, put those cans in the bin please," said Kyle, pointing to their litter.

"Who died and made you boss of me?" asked Nikau, sending his friends into fits of laughter.

"Bro, just do it," said Pania.

He jumped on the cans until they were flat and flung them like frisbees. They bounced off the bin.

"Epic fail!" said Ben, and Tipene cracked up.

Pania stood with her hands on her hips, glaring at Nikau. Acting mock-sheepish, he picked up the cans and drop-kicked them into the bin.

"Hop in guys. We need to get to Ohakune before the shops shut," said Pania.

As the van waited at the junction to the main road, a car indicated to turn right into the picnic site. It was a faded black sedan. It had an over-sized spoiler that would make the car airborne if lifted by a gale. As it crossed their path, Jabu noticed two men seated in the front. The driver looked ghostly. He had a pallid complexion and ash blonde hair. He stared into their van with more than passing curiosity. Jabu shivered. *Weirdo*, he thought but said nothing.

The van followed the outline of the still, blue lake, climbing an incline before leaving Lake Taupō behind them. Soon they were passing another lake and a gently rounded hill. Sulphurous smoke gushed from a geyser in the nearest mountain. Pania pulled the van up at a lookout point.

"You might want to take some pics," she offered.

It was scenic, but Jabu realised she had stopped for another reason.

"How about I tell you a story about how the mountains ended up where they are?" she asked.

"Sure," said Jabu.

"It has been passed down from my people." She pointed at the hill. "This is the first character in the legend. She is called Pihanga. Remind me to tell you later about how all the warrior mountains loved her and wished for her to be their wife."

"Interesting," said Jabu. "And what's that smoking mountain called? Is it a volcano?"

"Yep. That's Tongariro. He still erupts now and then…"

Jabu was gawking. He had never seen an actual volcano before.

Her eyes sparkled, revealing pride for her land and the stories passed on for generations.

Nikau had overheard the conversation. He hung his head out the van window and butted in. "Our *whakapapa* come from the Tūwharetoa tribe. Ma doesn't talk about it much, but Nana has told me many stories about our heritage."

"Yeah, we identify with our iwi and their relationship with the land. We sum it all up in a *pepeha*."

"I'd love to hear it," said Jabu.

In a soft and solemn voice, Pania spoke, *"Ko Tongariro te maunga, Ko Taupō te moana, Ko Tūwharetoa te iwi…"*

"That means, Tongariro is the mountain, Taupō is the lake and Tūwharetoa is the tribe," translated Nikau.

"You interrupted me again," said Pania. "He's well proud of his heritage," she said, turning to Jabu and Kyle.

"And I'm proud of my real Dad's Viking ancestors too," added Nikau, puffing out his chest.

Pania's expression changed to one of disapproval. It was fleeting, and well disguised, but Jabu had begun to tune into her facial cues. She quickly changed the subject.

"We'd better crack on," she said, climbing back into the van.

They drove on for a while, enjoying the ever-changing scenery. Red tussock and rocks dominated the landscape as they drew nearer to the distant mountains. Not much grew here, besides the adaptive grass, cradling herbs and flowers beneath its arching blades. Invasive heather vied for territory. Fiery eruptions in the past had prevented the regrowth of forests, even miles beyond the craters. Jabu gawked at the unfamiliar landscape as if he was a visitor to the moon. He let out a sigh of appreciation as the mountains loomed on their left.

That was a cue for Pania to pull over again. The younger boys and

Areta stayed in the van chatting, while Pania, Jabu and Kyle stepped out.

Two imposing snowcapped volcanoes claimed their timeless space side by side, leaving Jabu insignificant and awestruck.

"They are both parts of Tongariro, geologically. But that cone-shaped mountain to the right is called Ngāuruhoe," said Pania. "They are sacred to us."

Ngāuruhoe reminded Jabu of photographs he had seen of Mount Fuji in Japan, or of Kilimanjaro. It was flat-topped, with sheer, symmetrical slopes.

"Are we going to ski on that?" asked Kyle with casual bravado.

Pania laughed. "No. I wanted to introduce you to the next two characters in the story."

"What story?" asked Kyle.

"The story about how the mountains all ended up where they are."

"Right," said Kyle, distractedly.

"Ruapehu is the mountain we'll ski on. We'll spot it further down the track," she continued.

"Epic!" said Kyle. He stretched out his arms, breathed in the cold air, and yawned.

They stood for a minute admiring the immense geological land-scape that smoked and steamed out of vents, reminding Jabu that they were in an active volcanic terrain. He shuddered against the icy wind. The sun hung low, and the cobalt blue sky streaked with clouds as if a dry brush had whisked them across a canvas. At that moment, Jabu felt incredibly small, and in awe of his creator. He could understand why the mountains were considered sacred to the local iwi. They made him think of God. A bible verse played itself in his mind.

"For ever since the world was created, people have seen the earth and sky. Through everything God made, they can clearly see his invisible qualities — his eternal power and divine nature." [1]

He was grateful to be in this place, at this moment. He looked over at Pania, who was shivering. Her cheeks had flushed with cold. Without thinking, he impulsively reached out and put his arm around her and gave her a brief hug.

"Don't get cold," he said. Kyle shot him a strange look.

"I'm hungus," moaned Nikau, out the window of the van. "There are no takeaways out here in the wop wops. We'd better crack a move on."

"True," said Pania. "We'll cook up a feed at the bach."

Jabu didn't understand half of what they said. He was still learning the local lingo, but his heart felt stretched and he couldn't wipe a goofy grin off his face.

Half an hour later, they drove into the village of Ohakune. The small village was a winter wonderland of fresh snow. Jabu admired Mount Ruapehu in the near distance. The vast snowy slopes reflected the last rays of sunset in a rose-tinted hue.

"I can't believe we're going up there," he said, almost to himself.

Pania smiled and nodded. "Yep. Wait until you see the views from up there!"

Jabu wanted to pinch himself. "Just hope I can get down the mountain on skis, and not on a stretcher."

Pania chuckled. "You'll be right."

The newly acquainted friends spent half an hour throwing snowballs, making snow angels and building snowmen in the yard. Then, hungry and cold, they bustled indoors.

Compared to the grandeur of the natural surroundings, the bach was humble. There were two small bedrooms, one for the girls and a dorm for the guys. A tiny open plan kitchen and living area lead to a bathroom and a drying cupboard for their equipment. The temperature inside was no warmer than a freezer, but

Nikau worked swiftly and soon had a blazing fire going in the living area.

Jabu felt snug standing in the warm kitchen, looking out at the mountain. The snowy peaks were aflame with sunset. He shivered, despite being cosy and warm. The idea of skiing on this incredible peak seemed crazy, but he was always up for an adventure.

As he helped with dinner, he reminded himself to ask Pania about the Māori legend. He wanted to hear the rest of the story about how the mountains came to be where they are. Pania had introduced him to some of the characters, but not the plot. What had happened between Pihanga, Tongariro, Ngāuruhoe and Ruapehu? He felt a tingling excitement waiting for her tell him the story that meant so much to Pania and her ancestors.

---

1. Romans 1:20.NLT

9

LEGENDARY VOLCANIC BATTLE

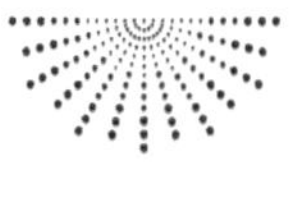

JABU

After dinner, Jabu felt lethargic. They all slouched on sofas and beanbags, listening to the sound of rain reverberating in the flue, and pattering on the tin roof. Higher up, on the maunga, that rain would be falling as snow. Pania spread out a ski resort map on the coffee table. She chartered their likely progression up the various runs. They would start off at the beginner-friendly 'Happy Valley' on the Whakapapa side of the mountain. Later, as they progressed, the group could tackle runs like "Boneyard," "The Giant" and "Vertigo." Pania said they could choose to either snowboard or ski.

"But before you decide which sport to learn, you need to know about the glacier challenge," said Pania. She unfolded a second map. This one was yellowed and held together with tape. As the group gathered closer, she pointed out a route across the top of the ski fields, marked out in red pen. It followed the circumference of the mountain before indicating a climb. She ran her finger down a valley. Jabu leaned in to read the valley's name on the map. He decided not to attempt a pronunciation.

"This is Mangatururu Glacier," said Pania, her voice full of salience.

"And?" asked Nikau.

"This is Papa Joe's map. These are his own hand-drawn directions to a remote glacial valley. Imagine no other skiers or boarders around and a free run down untouched snow."

"Sounds epic," said Kyle. "But it wasn't on the ski resort map. Is it only for advanced riders?"

"Yep. It's off-piste and gnarlier than a black run. And we'd have to use climbing skins to get there. That's why it suits skiers more than boarders. I'm giving you a heads up now, to give you all something to work towards. I wouldn't do it alone, but if any of you feel up to it at the end of our training, let me know. If not, you have plenty of other options."

Jabu listened attentively, picturing everything she said in vivid detail. The glacier. The untouched snow. A view from the top of the world, or so it sounded. Even the high altitude trek seemed like a worthwhile challenge. He resolved to make it his goal to join her.

"What are skins?" asked Tipene.

"They're strips that you attach to touring skis to help you climb slopes," said Pania. "They let the ski slide forward but not backward. Pretty cool."

"Climbing sounds tiring. I'm not bothered with all that. I might muck around on the terrain park rather," said Ben, yawning.

"Me too," agreed Tipene, giving Ben a fist bump.

There was a pause, as the rest of the group contemplated their options. Pania looked over at her younger brother expectantly. Jabu thought she looked like a quiz show contestant, hoping their teammate would make the right choice. Then Nikau spoke, and Pania's face fell.

"Na. Skiing is lame. I'll hang out with my boys and do some sick jumps, bro".

"Okay," said Pania with a sigh. "There's still time to decide, though."

It seemed to Jabu that she was reluctant to take no for an answer. Yet Pania handled her brother with the heedfulness of a tetchy cat's owner. He was all claws, and she coaxed.

To Jabu, she was regal. She carried herself up tall, like a Māori princess. He gazed over at her, stealing impressions while she was distracted. Her shiny black hair fell around an elegant long neck. A curling mouth softened her russet eyes, that seemed to hide a secret. Something that disturbed her peace.

After Nikau and friends had done the dishes with much splashing and clashing, towel whipping and messing, they ran out of restless energy.

Nikau yawned loudly. "I'm gonna crash."

"Yeah, time to hit the sack," said Ben, catching Nikau's yawn.

One by one, the group made their way to the bathroom and bed. Pania got up to brew herbal tea. Jabu fixed himself a hot chocolate before relaxing into a beanbag. After the others were beginning to snore and the fire was dying low, Jabu tried to pluck up the courage to speak to Pania. She had curled up on the couch with a book called *The Restless Land*[1]

"Pania," he said, "What happened with um, the mountains, you know, in the story you were telling me?"

She smiled and lowered her book to her chest. She stared at the drawn curtains as if looking beyond them to Mount Ruapehu.

"Ruapehu, Tongariro and Mount Taranaki are all restless volcanoes," she said. "Perhaps they are unsettled because —well, love does that."

"Ruapehu is extinct though, right?" asked Jabu.

"Nope," Pania said, and laughed, not unkindly.

"But... but we're going to ski on it?"

"Don't worry. It hasn't blown since 1945. It's resting now. We'll be fine."

"Eish!" said Jabu, eyes wide. "If you say so."

"Sometimes," she said, sounding whimsical, "the crater lake at the top gets so cold that it freezes over. We're in a warming phase at the moment, but scientists are monitoring it. I guess it would be in the papers if it were about to blow."

Jabu felt daunted. Wasn't skiing on an active volcano a bit reckless? But then, he'd never been the cautious type. He had joked about it with the children at Green Room House, but that was when he thought Ruapehu was sleeping. Pania's nonchalance lent her a fearless air that he found attractive.

"Right. Not sure how I'll sleep tonight, but please, carry on with the story." He grinned wryly.

"You'll be fine." She winked at him. At that moment Jabu decided that, volcano or not, he would follow her anywhere on the mountain. He leaned in closer and waited for her to carry on.

"Imagine a beautiful maiden, who has won the love of the great warriors, who have gathered around her," she said.

"I can't possibly," he said with a chuckle.

"Well, that gently sloped hill called Pihanga, was the desired bride. Her forest is like an emerald robe, draped around her. Now all the mountains were like gods. Tongariro was the chief. Taranaki, Tauhara, Putuaki and Ruapehu were among them. They all wanted to marry her, but she favoured Tongariro. A fiery battle took place — with heaving and earthquakes — eruptions and lava!"

"Who won?"

"Tongariro was victorious. The defeated mountains agreed to part ways. Tuahara and Putuaki decided to head towards the east. They said farewell to Pihanga. Ah, I need to read you this next bit." Pania paged through her book, paused, and began to read out loud:

"'They travelled all through one night. It was a magic pilgrimage during the hours of darkness; the only time when spirits and mountains can journey. Taranaki travelled fast and angrily and at daylight he halted at the sea coast where he now gazes towards the setting sun.'

I'll show Taranaki to you when we get up Ruapehu. You can see the top of his cone peaking up above the clouds..." She went back to reading.

"Puataki was halted by the dawn when he had travelled the greater part of his journey east." Her eyes skipped ahead, "'But Tauhara was the slowest of Pihanga's admirers. He travelled with tardy, lingering steps. He paused many times to gaze towards his lost love. When daylight came and stopped his march he had reached the place where he still stands, near the shores of Taupō Moana' — that's Lake Taupō, remember it?"

"Sure do."

"'He eternally looks back across the lake at the beautiful Pihanga.'"

Pania had a dreamy expression on her face. "Imagine being loved like that?" Then she caught herself. "Anyway, that's the story passed down by my people. There are different iwi and variations in the story. But when I come here, I always feel so connected to my roots. I love the stories. I love the *maunga*." She reached over and touched his hand. "I hope you will too." Then, unexpectedly, Pania climbed down from the couch and kissed Jabu on the cheek. "Night," she said. Jabu watched her glide into the bedroom, his cheek burning from her molten kiss. He cautioned himself not to be swept away by this princess and her land. *I have roots too*, he thought, remembering his Mama, his friends and the children at Green Room House.

Later, cocooned in a sleeping-bag, Jabu lay awake. He listened to the exotic bird-calls from the nearby forest. Finally, when he slept, he dreamed about skiing down a volcano, caught in the middle of an epic battle. Volcano gods spewed fiery balls at one another, while an ethereal princess stood, dressed in an emerald robe beside an azure lake, watching, hoping her beloved would win. Amid the earth-shattering chaos, he skied down cliff faces, dodging rock bombs, surfing avalanches and landing, finally, breathlessly at Pania Pihanga's bare feet.

---

1. Department of Conservation and Tongariro Natural History Society. 1998. *The Restless Land. Stories of Tongariro National Park World Heritage Area*. Everbest Printing Co., Ltd. 156p.

10

A GRACIOUS GIFT

JABU

The next morning, Pania drove the excited group to the Whakapapa side of Mount Ruapehu. Green farmland gave way to a rugged volcanic landscape. Clumps of snow took refuge in rocky shadows and the mountain loomed.

At the Visitor Centre, Jabu and friends learned about how Te Heuheu Tukino Horonuku had gifted the peaks to the Crown in 1887. Decades later, Tongariro National Park became a World Heritage Site. Pania and Nikau seemed proud, in a humble way. They were sharing their heritage, their ancestor's revered place, with the visitors. Jabu, sensing the significance of the moment, squeezed Pania's hand as she stood before the statue of Horonuku.

After the informative stop, the van wound its way up the flank of the mountain, to the ski fields. The group spent the day learning how to ski or snowboard on a long, gentle slope called 'Happy Valley'. The boarders fell over frequently, earning sore backs and icy bottoms for their efforts. The skiers spent hours learning how to do pizza-style snowploughs and controlled turns.

"My feet hurt like crazy," said Jabu, loosening his snowboot a notch.

"Well, you could be snowboarding," taunted Nikau. "My boots are comfy as…"

"Yeah, but look at your butt," laughed Jabu, pointing at the crusty layer of ice on Nikau's pants. Jabu had noticed that Nikau seldom fell over unless he was trying out a new manoeuvre. However, he still needed to sit in the snow to clip boots into bindings.

"One of the hazards," he said, dusting himself off with a shrug.

A friendly rivalry developed between the skiers and snowboarders. Nikau and Areta were teaching Tipene and Ben to snowboard, while Pania instructed Jabu and Kyle on skis. Competitiveness between the two groups spurred them on. Each swore that their chosen sport was superior. In an attempt to learn faster than the competing group, the beginners improved rapidly.

As the days went by, the learners progressed, from 'Happy Valley' to the narrow 'Rock Garden' track and beyond, to the far west runs.

The first lift on this progression spins around fast. Jabu learnt that getting onto a ski lift is an art in itself. He had not positioned himself properly, and half sat on the steel arm of the chair, sliding off and then hanging on to the seat. The chair dragged him a couple of metres before the operator pressed the off switch, bringing the lift to a halt. His left ski had unclipped and stood upright in the snow. The ski chairs swung back and forth as skiers looked grumpily over their shoulders. People in the queue seemed to be watching impatiently. He could have dug an underground igloo at that moment and crawled in. It was the most embarrassing moment of his life. But he stood up slowly, tried to smile, and clipped his boot back into his ski. Then he shuffled across the snow and slunk into the lift chair. He made up his mind to get it right, every single time from now on.

∽

After a week of intensive instruction, a blizzard halted their progress. Jabu was not alone in feeling relieved to rest his weary muscles for a couple of days.

The first clear day after the gale, Pania announced they were ready for the Turoa ski fields on the near side of the mountain. She drove the van through an almost endless forest of towering podocarp trees and ferns. Jabu imagined getting lost as he peered into the dense darkness. He wondered how you would find your way back to civilisation. He imagined that the trees and ferns would form an unforgiving maze. Jabu's outlook picked up once they surfaced above the forest line. Now they were immersed in a world of snow, radiantly reflecting the sunlight.

Jabu and Kyle began to take quantum leaps in skiing on their visits to Turoa. The young snowboarders had hit a plateau in their learning and were struggling. The 'Giant' run, with its sheer ploughed tracks and constricted 'boneyard' section, had them either braking most of the way or falling on their rears. Nikau, to his credit, stuck with his friends and patiently tried to show them the ropes.

One afternoon, Pania took Jabu and Kyle to the highest ski-lift accessible runs in Turoa. They paused on a ploughed ridge and looked out across the vista. A blanket of dazzling snow covered the mountain below them. Beyond it sprawled the forest and further still, on the horizon, a pointed cone peaked up above a sliver of cloud. The far distant mountain peak appeared to be floating — suspended like an inverted ice-cream cone.

"That's Taranaki," said Pania. "Remember the story?"

Jabu nodded. The mountain that had travelled furiously fast and had to stop when it reached the coast. He imagined Taranaki turning his back on Tongariro and Pihanga in a huff.

"I remember," he said, smiling.

Kyle glanced at them, sulkily. Then he bent down to adjust his ski boot, flicking the ice off the clip. Jabu wondered what was bugging Kyle, but needed to turn his attention to the sheer drop ahead of them. Jabu felt suitably terrified but did not want Pania to sense it. He took a deep breath and pulled his shoulders back.

"This track is called Vertigo," she said. "It's a black run. You'll need to watch out for the icy bits, and the death cookies."

"The what?" asked Jabu.

"You know, the cookie-sized chunks of ice," she explained.

"Is that all?" asked Kyle in a sarcastic tone.

"And other skiers and boarders of course. But just breathe in on the turns, exhale after them and try to enjoy it!"

Jabu knew this would be a muscle burner. But, like surfing a big wave, he was up for it. He followed Pania and Kyle, dropping off over the edge, and carved his way down the mountain. Cold air nipped his exposed neck but felt refreshing. The icy sections nearly slew him a couple of times, but he was focused and nimble. His surfing instincts kicked in. He felt courageous and bold, and within a few adrenaline-fuelled minutes, he had conquered the run. He came to a quick hockey stop in front of Pania, spraying her with snow. He had raced past Kyle, who came to a halt a minute later. Pania and Jabu pulled up their goggles and laughed with exhilaration.

"Epic!" said Pania. "A few more black runs and you guys will be ready to go off-piste. I have to say, you're both naturals."

"You're a good teacher," said Jabu, beaming. It wasn't the first time he had been called a natural, he thought.

"Yeah, thanks," grunted Kyle.

"No problem," she said. "Ready to do it again?"

Over the next two days, the three friends skied every black run in Turoa. Jabu felt at times as if he was flying. Experiencing this with Pania, made it all the more enjoyable. He loved how she was completely relaxed on the mountain. He made her laugh. He didn't know why. He didn't think he was funny, but she would throw her head back and laugh at his observations and comments. It made him feel as if their cultural difference was a point of richness.

He couldn't figure out why Kyle didn't seem to be enjoying himself, and when he asked what was wrong, his friend shrugged and said, "Nothing, dude."

Finally, the day came for them to go off-piste. Pania had promised to take Jabu and Kyle backcountry and teach them how to use skins. This would be the final preparation for the glacier challenge. The rest of the group planned to practice jumps at the terrain park lower down the mountain.

The van came to a halt at the base of the mountain road by an illuminated sign that read, "STOP. Turoa Closed Today. Check with Information Centre about re-opening."

"Far out!" said Nikau, throwing his hands in the air.

Pania made a sudden U-turn. "Let's go to the visitor centre and find out why it's closed."

"It's cloudy today — they might be struggling to de-ice the ski lifts," Areta suggested.

Jabu waited with the others in the van at the visitor centre. Pania came out looking as if she had been told that aliens had landed. She was shaking her head in disbelief.

"What is it, sis?" asked Nikau.

"There was an eruption this morning, shortly after eight o'clock." She looked stunned.

Jabu swung round to look at the mountain. Besides the sooty greyness of cloud cover, he couldn't make out anything distinctive. He held back as the group inundated Pania with questions.

Pania explained that the Turoa lift operators had seen a mudflow seeping out of the crater lake that morning. "Scientists are flying around the lake as we speak," she said, wide eyed. "They're investigating. The lady at the information desk reckons the mountain might well be closed for a few days."

"Ah, stink!" said Tipene.

"We can't forget where we are," said Pania. "We need to respect these ancient volcanoes. How about we go for a bushwalk near the village today instead?"

Ben groaned.

Jabu was surprised at how disappointed he felt. He had amped himself up for backcountry skiing with Pania. And yet, it was incredible that this giant mountain was rumbling. Reminding them of the potential for violence. They would have to be patient and hope Ruapehu would allow them onto his slopes again.

THE TAVERN

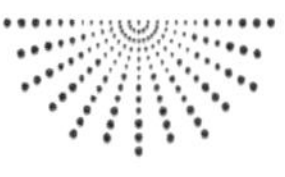

NIKAU

Nikau felt despondent, waking to the sound of heavy rain. He pulled the curtains open to look at his maunga. A swirling mass of cloud shrouded the mountain, suggesting a gale-force wind at high altitude. But then he remembered that even if it were clear, they wouldn't be boarding or skiing today. The ski-lift operators had closed the mountain because of the crater lake spill. He would have to hunker down with the others in the little railway bach until the storm passed.

"Ah bums," he said. He went into the living room and set about making a fire in the wood burner. *That'll get these lazy fellas out of bed,* he thought. They surfaced one by one and got to work. Pania and Jabu cooked breakfast together, scrambling eggs and grilling tomatoes and mushrooms. Kyle served plunger coffees while Areta washed last night's dishes.

After breakfast, Tipene strummed on his guitar. Nikau and Ben joined him for a while, singing melodic songs in a lively harmony. Next, they all joined in a game of Monopoly that sprawled across the coffee table. Jabu and Pania formed an underlying alliance which seemed to irk everyone.

Nikau kept the fire going as they all mooched about the bach. For lunch, they cobbled together a few sandwiches with leftover sausages and crisps. Then the snacks came out — chocolate, nuts and bikkies. Outside, the wind howled, and rain fell on and off. It began to snow again. The once smooth, white blanket on pavements, had turned into grey slush. Inside it was toasty. The fire crackled and blazed. It was all too settled for Nikau.

"I'm bored," grumbled Nikau. "And I'm missing the Piha party of the century tonight." He stood up clumsily, knocking his fake money to the floor.

"Give us your properties?" asked Tipene.

"Sure, I don't care…"

"That's not fair," piped Ben.

"Take my money then," said Nikau. He stood, arms folded, looming over Pania who padded the miniature iron across the board.

"Pass Go, two hundred dollars please," said Pania. She looked up at Nikau. "Yep?"

"I need one of the over eighteens to come with me to buy beersies."

Pania glared at him. "Don't go there, Nikau. You know the rules."

"The rules suck. I'm holed-up here, missing an epic party and playing dumb ass games. What d'ya say, boys? Beer time, right?"

Tipene glanced at Ben, who avoided his eye and flicked through the Monopoly money he had gathered off the carpet.

Pania spoke in a low, quiet voice. "Kitchen, now."

Nikau followed his sister to the open plan kitchenette, readying himself for confrontation.

"Ben just came out of rehab," she hissed. "And Tipene nearly got himself expelled last year. You know that. They're trying to come clean, and you're leading them astray."

"Aw, what's a couple of beers," said Nikau loudly.

Pania frowned and put her pointer finger to her lips. "They're addicts," she whispered, "and one beer leads to trouble. I can't believe you're so insensitive."

"Boy wants to have a good time," said Nikau, "and sister is a nun."

"Getting you all clean is the whole point of Aotearoa Ora Adventures!" said Pania, her hands on hips.

"Fancy name for sitting around playing kids games," huffed Nikau. "I'm going for some air." He unhooked his ski jacket from the drying rack in the entrance hall and charged out into the bracing dusk.

"Born in a stable!" shouted Pania after him, slamming the front door.

The wind had teeth, and Nikau was glad for his mountain jacket. He dug hands deep into jean pockets, pulled his beanie down low and strode towards the village. *At least this gale is bringing fresh powder*, he thought. He pined for the mountain and the free feeling of picking your way down a rocky slope. He thrived on being off-piste and in ultimate control. Without the adrenalin rush of snowboarding, the getaway was becoming oppressive. He felt like getting drunk and acting crazy. He crossed the road and wandered into a shop in Ohakune village.

At the supermarket till, a girl younger than him had the cheek of turning him away.

"No I.D., no alcohol," she said, barely opening her mouth to exercise her thin-lipped authority.

"Who died and made you president?" asked Nikau.

Outside the shop, he admired an orange Mustang with darkened windows, parked outside the local tavern. *Here goes nothing*, he thought, sauntering in.

The tavern was bigger inside than he had imagined. A brassy blond crooned into a microphone while a grey-haired rocker milked his electric guitar with remarkable skill. A haze of smoke hung in the air. Small groups gathered on barstools around raised tables, laughing and smoking over their glasses. Two men hunched over the bar counter, sipping on bourbon.

Nikau's legs felt like jelly, and his gut churned, but he strolled over and leaned on the broad kauri counter.

The barman came over, wiping a glass with a drying towel.

"No hoodies on in here mate," he said, affably.

"Sorry," said Nikau, pulling it back.

"What are ya after?"

"A pint of, erm, lager?"

"I.D."

"Oh, I don't have it on me, but I'm eighteen…" lied Nikau.

The man sitting closest to him had swung around, and he could tell from the corner of his eye that this man was eyeballing him.

"Don't worry, he's with me," said the man, standing and patting Nikau on the shoulder.

"Dad?"

Axel grinned at Nikau, seemingly delighted to see him. Nikau surprised himself by hugging his father.

The barman conceded to allowing Nikau one beer. Nikau gulped his pint, grinning.

"Thanks," he said, wiping a foamy moustache on the back of his sleeve.

"All good mate," said Axel. The burly man beside him leered over at them curiously. Axel did not introduce him, focusing his attention on Nikau. "Good to see you, my boy," he said, ruffling Nikau's hair.

"So, what're you doing in Ohakune?" asked Nikau, trying to remember if he had told Axel he was coming skiing. Had his Dad come to find him so that they could spend time together?

"Oh, me and Vito here are doing some sightseeing now we're…" he lowered his voice, "now we're both out."

Vito nodded his square head, turning the sides of his mouth down in affirmation. It reminded Nikau of the expression the mafia used in movies.

"It's helluva good luck that we've bumped into you," said Axel, beaming. "So what're you doing in a tavern?"

Nikau had swallowed down the pint and began to offload his frustration to his father.

"All I wanted was to skull a few beers. I'm missing a big party tonight while Pania and her pet projects sit around singing kumbaya, playing board games and drinking tea…"

"Oh, don't worry son, I've got a whole crate in the boot of the car," said Axel, sliding a note across to the barman and standing to go. He shepherded Nikau out the door, a hand heavy on his shoulder. Vito unlocked the boot of the orange muscle car, pulling out the beers. Axel opened the back door and gestured for Nikau to climb in.

Vito fired up the engine. It growled.

"Wow, this beast has grunt!" said Nikau.

"You've seen nothing," said Vito, flooring it. The car surged forward, accelerating instantly, but Axel whispered, "Don't get us pulled over."

Vito braked abruptly and eased along the main street at a snail's pace while the engine grumbled in frustration. He turned left at a T-junction and floored it again, levelling out at the local speed limit of one hundred. The car purred along the open road for a few kilometres.

"Where are we headed?" asked Nikau.

"Just here," said Vito, pulling the car into a picnic spot. He turned off the engine, parking under a tree. Axel threw Nikau another beer.

It felt thrilling drinking beers in the dusk with two ex-jailbirds, in a dream car, and even more exciting that one of them was his Dad. Nikau grinned a silly, self-satisfied smile.

After a few beers, Axel began to tell funny stories from prison. He was a hard case. Nikau laughed like a hyena at his Dad's jokes. Axel's slight Scandinavian accent gave his words a quirky edge, adding to the humour of his tall tales. Next, Vito had pulled out a bottle of hardtack and shooter glasses. Before he knew it, the sun had set, and he was drunk, in a car with two ex-convicts, and he had not yet begun to feel unsafe.

12

A FORTUNATE ACCIDENT

NIKAU

Nikau sensed the mood in the car had changed as the last light faded.

"When ya gonna ask him?" nudged Vito.

Axel's expression changed, laughter dropping from his face in an instant. He nodded and turned to the back seat. He leaned over the chair and looked Nikau directly in the eyes.

"Son, you have something of mine, don't ya?"

Nikau squirmed under the fixed, cold gaze.

"Say what?"

"Now come on, boy, don't make me spell it out. Where have you hidden it?"

Nikau remembered the ziplock bag that he had thrown in the trash outside. He couldn't remember what day they collected the trash, but it was more than likely in a rubbish dump by now. He felt sick with the realisation that he had done something irreversible.

"I, I dunno what you mean…"

Axel spoke slowly now. "What… else was in the tin?"

Nikau shrugged. "Nothing. I mean, I never opened it."

"Liar," spat Vito. "Don't mess with us," he said, jumping halfway out his seat and grabbing Nikau by the collar of his jacket. Vito pulled him close choking Nikau on his collar.

"Put him down!" yelled Axel.

"It's my stash too, and I've had enough of this bull," growled Vito, glaring at Axel with hatred.

"You'll get what's yours. Trust me," said Axel as if placating a beast.

Nikau reached for the door handle, but Axel leaned back and placed his hand over his son's. He held it there and spoke quietly.

"It's alright, son. Look, no need to scarper off anywhere, we'll drive you back to your bach now, won't we Vito?"

"Sure boss," said Vito, with fake-deference.

The engine growled into life. They cruised along the open road, back to the village. They seemed to be taking a scenic route. Nikau decided not to give them the address of the railway bach.

"Jus' drop me in the village," slurred Nikau, as the alcohol caught up with him. He felt woozy.

Vito studied Axel, who nodded.

"Sure son. Sorry about the misunderstanding, eh."

"No worries… hope ya find what you're looking for," garbled Nikau, finding it hard to keep his eyes open. His head was spinning. At least they believed him, for now. He didn't know what Vito would do if he discovered Nikau had turfed their treasure. He rested his head back on the comfy leather headrest. Within minutes the purr of the engine lulled him into an inebriated slumber.

When Nikau awoke, he startled to find he was in a car, with what felt like two strangers. Their deep voices rumbled in conversation. He listened for a while as he woke.

"Remember, I own half of the earnings for that stash. Your cocky little squirt better tell us where it is or…" Vito complained.

"Or what?" said Axel. "Look, don't get all threatening on me. He'll show us where it is. He probably hid it somewhere on his property. We'll interrogate him, soon as we get to Auckland."

"I'll interrogate him with my knuckles if he doesn't fess up," said Vito.

Axel yawned and bit into an apple.

"How much d'ya reckon it's worth now? On the street?" asked Vito.

"Hmm, maybe fifty K."

"Na, you're trying to undersell me. It's worth at least a hundred."

"We'll see," said Axel, with finality.

"What if he tells the cops?" asked Vito, getting agitated again.

"He won't. He dug up the tin, hid the stash — he's an accomplice drug dealer. We'll remind him of that." At this, both men laughed loudly, then quietened so as not to wake him.

"Shh," said Axel.

Nikau lay still, feigning sleep-breathing, his eyes open a slit. His heart raced, but his body felt frozen. Outside the world chased past, pitch black. He tried to look for street signs to give him an idea of where he was, but it was dark. Rural. Vito was racing like a bullet and none too sober. *Dumb ways to die*, thought Nikau bitterly. His chances of getting anywhere safely felt slim at this rate. And if he survived a kidnapping by a drunk driver, he would have to deal with owning up that the stash was turfed out.

"Here, have a swig to calm your nerves mate," said Axel, passing a small glass bottle across to Vito. The road veered left at that moment. The bright lights of a timber truck flashed into view as Vito reached for the rum, allowing the car to drift across a double yellow line. They were on the brink of a head-on collision when Nikau yelled out. Axel grabbed the steering wheel, pulling the car sharply over to the left, away from the truck. As the tyres dug into a muddy shoulder, Vito hit the brakes hard. They careened through snow and mud, bouncing to a stop, crashing into a wooden fence. Nikau heard the horn of the truck blasting as the enormous vehicle raced past in the opposite direction. In the impact, Nikau's safety belt had stopped him from colliding with the driver's seat. For a moment, there was nothing but the sound of the engine idling.

Axel groaned and clambered out. He traipsed through the mud towards Nikau's door, flinging it open. He stared blankly, his pale eyes registering no emotion.

"Good. You're alive."

He left Nikau in the back seat and walked around to the driver's seat, where Vito was now screaming in pain.

"I've broken my leg!" he cried out.

Axel walked back to Nikau, unstrapped his seatbelt and grabbed him roughly by the wrist.

"Get up. Walk with me," Axel instructed. He marched away from the accident with Nikau stumbling behind him, disoriented.

"What are you doing? What about Vito?"

"Shut up," said Axel, continuing until they were a long way up the road. He pulled out his brick-sized mobile phone, punched in a number and waited. "Yes, emergency… Car accident… Ambulance and police… Yes, they almost collided into me. I managed to see the number plate. Yes, it was JT6484… No, we didn't stop, I have children with me, but I can tell ya it's on State Highway 4. Near Smash Palace. No kiddin' — a stolen car, eh? Sheez, well I hope you catch that fella and lock him up. We don't want those sorts on the roads… My name? Look, I can't hear you, I seem to have lost signal." He hung up. In the yellow light of a nearby lamppost, Nikau distinctly saw Axel grinning to himself.

"What was that about? We need to go back, to help Vito," said Nikau, grabbing Axel's arm.

"Noooooo way. He's cooked his goose. They'll lock him up for a long time now. And I won't have to give him fifty percent of the spoils."

"What? You're sick, man," said Nikau.

"Hey, I might even be able to give you a share, as soon as you hand it over. Now come, we'll hitch a ride to Auckland, and you can take me to my goods."

"You're a crazy man! Are you not even loyal to your best mate? I mean, I can't say I like the guy, but didn't he stand by you all those years in the trunk?"

"What of it?" said Axel, pulling the finger at a car that drove past them without stopping.

"And now you're setting him up?" The shock of the accident, and the icy breeze on his face, had sobered Nikau. His thoughts were racing. Finally, his emotions welled over.

"You're a heartless, selfish… I can't believe you're my father!"

"Why not? You're not unlike me, you know. From what I can see, you're pretty disloyal y'self. Digging up a tin in your stepdad's yard, hiding your old man's stash and lying about it. What else? Ah, drinking against your sister's will. Hell fella, it looks like you don't answer to anyone but your's truly. It's the best way to be really. You'll soon find out. It's a cold, hard world, my boy."

13

SMASH PALACE

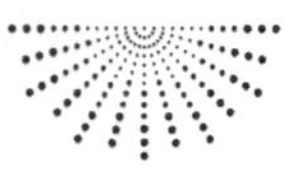

NIKAU

Standing beside his backstabbing father at the edge of State Highway 4, Nikau realised he had been a fool. Axel was not turning out to be anything like the father for whom he had pined. The man had shown himself to be without conscience. A hand clenched Nikau's wrist, preventing him from running back to help Vito.

"Come on, boy, stop tugging against me," Axel said, as a car cruised past them. "Cut me some slack."

Nikau wanted to rail against him. To tell him what a disappointment he was. To beg for them to turn back and help Vito, even though he feared the man. He could refuse to go to Auckland. To tell Axel, this was tantamount to a kidnapping. But his street smarts made him go silent instead. He weighed his options, and a plan began to take shape.

"Alright, alright, you win!" said Nikau. He picked up the pace, matching his father stride for stride along the isolated road. He pretended to cooperate. After a time, Axel released the grip on Nikau's wrist. Axel shoved his thumb out at an approaching sedan. Nikau plunged himself into a bush before the lights of the car could

70

illuminate him. The luxury car slowed down, pulling over to the shoulder. Axel's attention focused on getting a ride and he had not noticed that Nikau had slipped away. The electric window slid down. His father stepped forward to address a man in a suit.

"Where you headed?" asked the businessman.

"Auckland, please," said Axel.

"Well, I could do with some company. But the question is, will you like my taste in music?" The man chuckled at his joke.

Axel laughed. "Anything goes, as long as it keeps ya awake."

"You're not dodgy, or anything are you?" asked the businessman.

"Na, just a regular bloke," said Axel, sounding earnest.

As they spoke, Nikau watched from his hiding place. Axel climbed into the front seat, slamming the door closed. As the car accelerated off, Axel turned to look over his shoulder at the back seat. Realising what Nikau had done, his expression was a mixture of shock and fury. The car soon disappeared down the long, dark road in the black night.

Nikau wouldn't have long. Axel would soon ask the driver to stop. Then he would be fast at his heels. Nikau bolted across the road. An ambulance sped towards him in the opposite lane, siren wailing. Without thinking, he sprinted in front of the ambulance to the other side of the road. He slid on loose gravel at the far shoulder, ripping jeans and grazing his left leg. Without stopping, Nikau ran towards the ghostly shape of the snowy mountain, glowing under a waxing moon. He climbed over a wooden fence and stumbled through a field. He tripped over the uneven ground and fell to his face in slush. Before Nikau could scramble to his feet, something rammed into him with brutal force. "Oomph!" he heard himself cry as he landed stomach first on a mound of dirt. A shadowy figure charged at him again. He heard bleating, not far off. *It must be a bloody ram*, he thought, rolling sideways. Hooves splashed passed his face as he ducked his head between elbows. He wanted to scream at the animal in dominance, to chase it away, but that would give away his location. Instead, Nikau lay still in the snowy mud, waiting for the ram to lose interest. With a victorious bleat, the alpha male scurried on. Nikau ran again, towards the mountain, away from the main road. He stumbled through the field, scattering a herd of startled sheep.

What will Axel do? he wondered. Surely his father wouldn't want to get caught near the stolen muscle car. And he would have seen the ambulance. Police couldn't be far off. Asking the businessman to stop and let him out would raise questions. Perhaps Axel would go back to Auckland and give up on the idea of getting the stash back. But then again, if he were desperate enough, he would stop the car and run after Nikau. *Did he see which direction I went?* Nothing was certain. Nikau decided to assume the worst and kept on running. He hoped to come across a farmhouse. With all these sheep around, there had to be a farmer. He staggered through the night.

Nikau reached the cemented mound of a train track that runs around the mountain. He tried to cross swiftly, but tripped over the first track, falling to his knees. Then he heard a rumble accelerating towards him. The light of the train was far in the distance, but approaching at speed. He climbed to his feet as the hooter shrieked with a plaintive cry. Nikau staggered forward, tripping over the second track and falling into a heap at the bottom of the mound. He watched in terror as the freight train rolled past. He had not seen the face of the driver, but he imagined it. Shock replaced by relief. *Alive. Dead.* It can happen in a fraction of a second. *Alive.*

Thankful to have been spared, Nikau continued his scramble through the night. It was too dark to tell if he was being tailed, but the train whistle would have given his location away. He broke into a trot. Then, in the distance, Nikau made out a jumble of shapes, dimly illuminated by the moon. He remembered Smash Palace! He had often wanted to go there, but Papa Joe had always refused to stop off on the way to Ohakune. It was a graveyard of vintage cars and trucks. The rusting skeletal shells were like monuments to the grandeur of days gone by. They signified a stubborn hope that someday these hulks might be resurrected. Stripped of steering wheels, hubcaps and grills, the cars possessed a resigned dignity. Nikau had often wished he could browse the shed. It was renowned for being chocka with parts. But tonight, he shuddered as he approached. A dog barked in the distance. The air smelled of oil and rubber tyres. Nikau crept forward, hands outstretched until he bumped up against a rugged steel form. His hands padded the outside of a rust riddled shell and felt a gaping hole where a glass window had been. He ran his hands down to a handle. Nikau pulled at it and stumbled back as the door fell away. He climbed in and pulled the door up against the gaping hole. It was an unexpected comfort to collapse on the worn leather seat. Nikau slumped down out of sight. *Axel might have a torch*, he surmised. If he lay below the window line, he may be able to catch his breath and order his thoughts. Once the panting had stopped, Nikau shivered. He hardly dared to breathe, listening for footsteps. How long would he need to hide in a rusty relic, under a moonlit mountain, in the depths of night?

14

FROM THE RUINS OF A RELIC

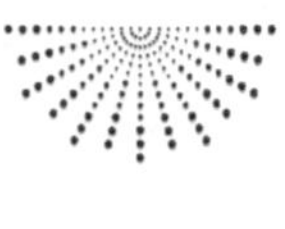

NIKAU

Nikau curled up for a time until his breathing was even and his heart rate had slowed. The cold night chilled him the longer he remained still. He pulled his knees up to his chest in a pitiful huddle. He lay like this for what felt like hours, listening.

His thoughts fell upon the car in which he hid. The rusty frame was like a cicada shell. A remnant. He imagined something grand, back in its heyday. A vintage classic Rolls Royce or Cadillac, a Buick or a Ford. Or a 1930s automobile once owned by the 'Great Gatsby'. He pictured the canary yellow paint, shining grill and proud mascot. He could hear the purring engine and smell leather and polish. But now, it was a wreck. Beyond repair.

The metaphor made him think of his Dad. Nikau had painted a picture in his mind of a man with potential. He had believed his father had fallen into a dark place but was not beyond redemption. When Axel came out of prison, Nikau had thought he would try to be a new man. Nikau would love him, and with enough care, he would make his Dad as good as new. That is what he had imagined before today. His Dad was like this car. Someone hoped they could fix it up, work on the rusty body, replace parts, but slowly they had realised that it was… irreparable. Was his father like that?

Axel had shown himself to be without conscience. Could his cold heart thaw? Nikau doubted it. A deep sadness fell over him. The loss of what could have been. He realised that time with his father would only rob him of any innocence that remained. He had no power to rescue his father from a life of crime, but he could avoid being thrown further into the thick of it.

Nikau jumped to attention, switching from metaphors to reality in a jarring instant. Something was scratching the door. Scriiiiiitch, scritch. He slunk down to the floor of the vehicle and curled up like a wombat. He heard himself mewl in fright. This was met by excitable barking. He sat still, petrified as the dog barked and scratched and jumped at the door. The unattached door fell with a clang to the ground, and the dog ran away, tail between legs, whimpering. Then it turned and skulked back, head below shoulder blades and tail low. It growled at Nikau, and he could not pretend to be invisible any longer.

"It's okay buddy," Nikau said in a soothing voice. "Good dog."

Surprisingly, the dog relaxed and began to wag a tail, tentatively.

"There's a good dog," said Nikau from his curled up wombat position. The dog barked again, but this sounded more like hello. Then it walked right up to the gaping hole, treading on the fallen door and prodded Nikau with a wet nose.

Nikau laughed. He loved dogs, and though he had never owned one, he had always been chummy with his friends' pets. The dog sniffed his flattened palm. Nikau raised himself on his palms onto the seat. The dog had become silly friendly now, wagging a thumping tail and licking him. She was a girl dog, he decided, although he could not tell in the dark. He assumed she was accustomed to all the comings and goings at Smash Palace. Trained to be a customer-friendly dog, not a guard dog. He sighed with relief.

Without warning the dog leapt, bouncing off him and landing on the opposite seat. She spun around in circles a handful of times before settling in a twirl, laying her head on his lap. Nikau was grateful. He had felt so alone and afraid until she came. He stroked the dog's soft head, and she licked his hand again.

"That's kinda gross, but okay," he whispered. "Well, if your owner hasn't come by now, I reckon he's slept through this eh?"

The tail thumped.

Feeling warmer with a dog to pet, Nikau relaxed and tried to think rationally about his situation. By now he was certain Axel had resigned himself to continuing back to Auckland. The ambulance would have taken Vito to the hospital by now. He guessed police would be investigating the report of a stolen vehicle. He hoped.

Nikau stroked the dog's silky ears, considering his options.

"Should I tell Pania everything?" he asked the dog.

Thump, thump.

"But she'll make me report Axel to the police," he whispered to the night.

He might be a sociopath, but I still don't want him going to jail again. Plus, Pania will tell Papa Joe, and I'll probably get expelled for digging up the tin. Even worse, I could go to jail for conspiring with a dealer, he thought. But he didn't tell the dog that.

She licked his hand and nudged him for another cuddle. He stroked her soft head thoughtfully.

"I'd better keep it a secret, girl."

Thump, thump went the tail. It seemed she liked his voice.

One secret had piled on top of another. Nikau had a mountain of secrets, like the maunga looming above them. He looked up towards Mt. Ruapehu. It surprised him to see the lights of snowploughs moving around up high, as they smoothed out fresh trails for the morning.

"The ski lifts must be opening tomorrow!" he sang out to the dog.

It cheered him up when he imagined the freedom of snowboarding. So far removed from here. Even Pania's glacier quest seemed appealing.

"I need to do something to get into my sister's good books," whispered Nikau, "instead of being a rotter like my Dad." *And anyway, the top of the mountain is about the safest place to be right now*, he thought. As far away from Axel as he could imagine.

"Sweet girl, I'm gonna have to say see ya. I'm gonna walk through the night if I have to, back to Ohakune. Or I'll get lucky and hitch a ride." Saying the words out loud gave power to his thoughts.

He ruffled the dog's fur. She pressed a cold nose against his hand, lifting her head from his lap as he began to rise.

"Thanks, pup. You're a good listener."

The dog hopped out the wreck and followed him as he slunk stealthily back the way he had come.

"Go home," he said, fighting back sadness.

She turned and wandered back to the car wreck yard, tail low, but wagging.

Nikau retraced his steps. The night had cleared allowing the waxing moon to cast a dim light, illuminating his path. Above him, the milky way spread out in a magnificent arc. For a moment, he almost felt peaceful. He stopped at the train line, checking left and right before crossing. He bolted through the field, hoping to avoid another altercation with the ram. This time, as it approached him, he raised his arms and yelled, scattering the ram and the flock. Then he limped along the main road towards Ohakune. His grazed thigh ached. He landed one foot in front of the other and hoped for a vehicle. There would be scarce traffic this late, on this lonely road. Nikau walked, parallel to the moonlit maunga, often gazing at the stars above. He walked away from his dreams of having a relationship with his real Dad. Every step he took made him feel a little less like a boy, and more like a man. From now on, every action was a choice.

When he felt he couldn't walk another step, a sports car pulled over.

"Where you headed?" asked a purple-haired woman. She reminded him of his nana.

All his manliness dissolved, and he replied in a quaking voice, "I'm trying to get back to my sister in Ohakune, miss."

"Hop in then, but be quick — my daughter is having a baby!"

The groovy granny poured out her family dramas to him, not once asking why he was walking State Highway Four alone, at night. He heard about her daughter's previous pregnancies and how this one was irregular. Her labour had come on suddenly, and now Gran hoped to get to Whanganui before the head crowned. It was too much information, but he listened politely and pressed an imaginary brake to the floor as she put pedal to the metal. Even so, the kindly woman went out of her way to drop him at the front door of the railway bach. He thanked her and wished her daughter all the best, before treading up the garden path. He tried the door. It was unlocked, so he snuck in, hoping all were asleep. The sound of deep breathing lent comfortable somnolence to the house. He switched on the kitchen light to get a glass of water, waking Pania, who had nodded off on the couch.

She sat up and rubbed her eyes.

"Nikau?" she asked, half asleep.

"Hi," he said, walking over to plant a kiss on her forehead. He stopped himself short, not wanting her to smell alcohol on his breath.

"What time is it?"

"Oh, not late," he replied.

"I called the cops!" she said, starting to awaken, "But they wouldn't let me report a missing person until after 24 hours. I was so worried about you." She seemed too bewildered to be angry. "Where did you go?"

"Just walking. And thinking. I'm sorry sis, I won't do it again. I promise." He tried to smile serenely at her, to show her something of the new man he felt he was becoming. "Get some sleep," he said, as if in charge.

Pania looked at him with relief and exasperation. "Thank God you're okay," she whispered. "If I wasn't so tired I'd be giving you a rark up. Do this again and I'll be taking you back to Auckland, eh."

"I won't," he assured her.

"Night then," she said, pulling the sleeping bag up and rolling over to face the back of the sofa.

He was back with his sister and friends, and all was right with the world. Tomorrow would be a new day.

15

STRANGER ON THE SKI LIFT

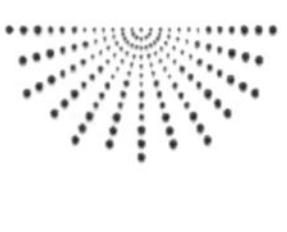

JABU

Two days later, the ski fields re-opened. The mountain had not erupted after the crater mudflow. Undeterred by the low risk of volcanic activity, the group headed up to the ski fields. Pania reckoned chances of the volcano blowing when they were on the slopes were slim. They were as likely to be hit by a bus, she had said. Today was a clear day, perfect for backcountry skiing and boarding. Fresh snow had fallen. It was what skiers call a 'bluebird day'. The brilliant white mountain appeared to be pasted onto a lapis lazuli sky. The towering peaks, stark and regal in contrast to the endless expanse of blue.

Jabu chose to head up the mountain with Kyle and Pania. They were eager to continue working towards the glacier challenge. Surprisingly them at the last minute, Nikau had announced that he wanted to join them in practicing on the upper slopes. Pania suggested he ski, to brush up his rusty skills. He insisted on snowboarding though.

"If you can ski it, I can board it," he said, arms folded.

The rest of the group snowboarded on the blue runs.

The Giant lift seated three, so Nikau shuffled ahead of the others in the queue. As they edged forward, a man pushed in front of Jabu from the left lane, almost knocking him off his skis. He seemed eager to get on the lift in a hurry. The man queued up next to Nikau. Jabu had not seen his face as he had a beanie and mask on. Yet, he recognised the tall man's camouflage ski pants and olive green jacket. He had noticed the skier down in the car park earlier, getting out of the same souped-up car he had seen in Taupō. Jabu was almost sure he was the same man who had leered into their van as they pulled out from Five Mile Bay. He felt strangely uncomfortable.

As the ski lift pulled away and accelerated upwards, Jabu noticed that the man had sidled up next to Nikau on the ski chair. The man's body language seemed threatening, while Nikau shook his head. Jabu turned to Pania and was about to ask her if she knew who the man was when the next lift spun towards them and they had to position themselves. Jabu was not going to reenact the most embarrassing moment of his life when he had been dragged by the lift chair. He was all focus at the ski lifts, with a cool cat veneer.

On the lift, he was distracted by the scenery, and by Pania. Her muscular thigh pressed against his leg. *Ski pants suit her*, he thought shyly. He looked down at the mountainside way below them. The slopes buzzed with skiers and snowboarders who careened down, oblivious of one another. Pint-sized toddlers in pink ski suits, zigzagged in full 'pizza' position, with no poles. Beginner snowboarders drifted noisily down slopes, out of control. Advanced skiers picked their way between them as if they were computer-generated hazards in a game. It amazed Jabu that there weren't more accidents.

Soon Jabu and friends were on the slopes, laughing and racing one another. They skied for hours, getting braver in modest increments and quantum leaps — pushing their comfort zones. After a challenging day of skiing, hiking on skins and snowboarding off-piste, the group of four gathered for a feed at Giant Cafe. Kyle carried over a tray laden with coffees, hot chocolates and chips.

"Chur," said Pania, pulling off her gloves.

Nikau's question came like a bolt of lightning on a clear day.

"Can we do the glacier quest thingie tomorrow?"

Pania looked taken aback. "I didn't think you wanted to do it?"

"I do. Tomorrow."

"Well, it depends on the conditions, they need to be right. Why tomorrow?"

"It has to be tomorrow. I don't want to be in the village anymore." He stared up at the maunga and pointed. "I want to be high up on the mountain, away from it all!"

"Well, it depends…"

"Please, sis! It's important." He looked as if he was about to cry. His legs shook under the table.

Jabu wondered if Nikau's outburst had anything to do with the dodgy-looking man in the camo pants. He blurted, "You're looking stressed out, buddy. This hasn't got anything to do with that fella on the ski lift?"

Nikau stared at him.

"What fella?"

"Uh," Jabu felt himself wilting under Nikau's fierce gaze. "A tall, pale-looking fella with camo pants… I saw him in Taupō… and then on the ski lift with you."

"So?"

"He seemed suspicious to me," finished Jabu.

"What the hell? You're spying on me now? I have an everyday convo with a bloke from Tauranga about the weather, and you start mistrusting a bro? That's not cool."

"I, uh, I'm concerned for you. Are you in trouble?"

Nikau shook his head and sighed. "I'm amazed you took your eyes off my sister for long enough to notice…"

"Nikau, apologise!" said Pania. "You're being rude."

"Whatever," said Nikau. "I'm gonna snowboard the half-pipe and then head up to High Noon."

"What about your chips?" asked Pania. He shrugged, picked up his snowboard and skulked away. He ambled across the snow, dragging his board behind him. Then he stopped, turned and came back to the table.

"Actually I am in some kind of trouble," he confessed. "I can't go into it and don't ask me to, okay. Just know that I'm struggling with something."

"And going on the glacier quest will help you deal with your feelings?" asked Pania.

"Yep. I guess," he said, turning to go.

Jabu and Pania, were sitting face to face, sharing a box of chips.

"I'll go with him," Kyle offered. "You two seem cozy." Nikau was out of earshot now. Kyle lowered his voice. "I'll keep an eye on him. See you guys down at the car park in an hour?"

Pania looked at her watch.

"Perfect, thanks."

Jabu and Pania watched as Nikau strapped his boots into his bindings and Kyle clipped on his skis. They dropped off over the ridge beyond the cafe tables, gliding down to the half-pipe bowl and out of sight.

Jabu and Pania found themselves alone together at this cafe halfway up the mountain. Icicles hung from the eaves like giant stalactites. The cafe heaved with hungry skiers, so they sat at a table out front, in the snow. Ahead of them, the view stretched out as far as Taranaki. Jabu couldn't help thinking that it would be a top-of-the-world setting for a first date — if only Pania wasn't upset.

A tear rolled down her cheek, and she ran a finger underneath her sunglasses to wipe another away.

"He's always in some kind of trouble, that boy. I brought him down here to clear the cobwebs, but now he's talking crazy!"

"He'll be okay. He needs to blow off some steam," said Jabu.

"What were you asking him about a dodgy bloke? I wasn't following?"

Jabu paused. He toned down his reply to avoid upsetting her further, "I noticed a shady looking man shoving his way onto the ski-lift with your bro. He seemed shaken after that."

"I wonder if he owes someone money?" she said as if she knew the answer.

"Well, whatever it is, let's try to get up the mountain tomorrow. Maybe that will give him a fresh perspective on things. He may even open up to you in that environment."

"Think so?" Pania stared out at the vista. "I worry so much. He's just like his father sometimes. Short-tempered. Impulsive."

She pulled her sunglasses up onto her forehead and lifted his, making eye contact.

"I want to share something with you," she said. She pulled off his glove and held his hand in hers. Then she began to tell him the story about her father, and the day he left them.

16

THE DAY AXEL LEFT

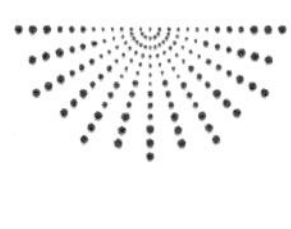

JABU

"I call him Axel," Pania began.

"I refuse to refer to him as Dad. He was very controlling. Ma was scared of him because he drank too much. I remember the day he hit her in the face. I was about six. Cute as pie," said Pania, a weak smile softening her expression for a moment. "Ma confronted him about his drinking. And she also accused him of taking drugs. It was the first time I had heard the word, 'drugs'. Ma was unusually challenging, and Axel snapped."

Pania breathed deeply, lowering her eyes.

"He punched her, right in the eye, and she fell against the kitchen bench."

Jabu shook his head, listening.

"I screamed at him and stood between them as he raised his fist again. 'Out of my way,' he said to me and pushed me aside. He couldn't have known how light I was because I flew in the air and landed in a crumpled heap in the corner. Ma dragged herself up and screamed out the window, 'Help us! Joe, Please… help!'"

"Who is Joe?" asked Jabu gently.

85

"The one I call Papa Joe. He's my step Dad now, but in those days he was the widower who lived next door. He was a private man. Kept to himself. Anyway, Joe was in the back yard, hanging up his laundry. Thank God. He rushed over, ran down the passage and pulled Axel off Ma. Axel was shaking her and screaming at her like a madman."

Pania's breathing had quickened. She appeared to be reliving the nightmare.

"Thank the Lord, Joe got there quickly," said Jabu.

"Too right. Papa Joe is a colossal man. With one strong arm, he pulled Axel by the shirt, away from Ma, and held him there. When Joe let go, Axel charged at them. Papa Joe stuck out his arm, like he was fending a rugby tackle, and gave him a gentle shove. Perhaps he didn't know his strength,' coz Pa is a gentleman, but Axel stumbled backwards, falling over. Then Papa Joe wrapped Ma and me in a warm, protective hug, like a giant bear. I felt so safe, and silently wished at that moment, that I could swap Axel for Joe. I wished he could be my Dad. And now, he is."

"Wow, that's heavy. And where was Nikau when this happened?" asked Jabu.

Pania wiped away another tear. Her guise had come off, and he could see her pain. In her moment of vulnerability, he felt even closer to her. She reminded Jabu of himself as a young orphan. Broken, but courageous.

"Nikau was so little," she continued. "About three or four, I guess. He arrived at the ranch slider holding a toy digger limply by his side. He had been digging in the mud under our back tree. Joe told Axel to get out. Axel scooped up Nikau and headed for the door." Pania began to cry.

Jabu moved over to her side of the bench and put his arm around her.

"It's okay now," he said.

She shuddered, taking short intakes of breath and wiping away salty tears with a ski glove. Jabu held her.

"Don't hold in your sadness," he said, letting her cry.

"My snot is turning to ice," she blubbered. She laughed and snorted. Jabu passed her a serviette.

"I… I thought Axel was going to leave with Nikau. I thought I would never see my little brother again, but then Ma screamed in the fiercest voice I've ever heard."

"What did she say?"

"She said, 'Put him down now you low life! I'm calling the cops.' And she did. They came and interviewed her. I don't know all the ins and outs, but to cut a long story short, she got a trespassing order against him. He's not allowed near any of us. They got divorced, and then he went off the rails. He started taking P and dealing in hard drugs. Ended up in prison." Pania sighed. "As far as I know, he's still in there. I just… I worry Nikau will end up like him."

"Does Nikau remember his Dad, uh, Axel?" asked Jabu.

"Yes, he does. But he has some idealised version of a loving father. Ma never let me tell him different. She didn't want him to know he had 'rotten genes'. 'That way,' she said, 'he'd have a better chance of turning into a good man. Like Papa Joe.'"

Jabu was silent. He tried to think of the right response to Pania's revelation.

"Damn, my coffee is cold," she said, pulling a face.

"I'll get you another."

"No. No. It's fine. Iced coffee," she said, trying to joke. She slurped it down. "Chip?"

They finished the remaining chips in silence.

Finally, Jabu spoke. "I'm so sorry that happened. That must have been rough on you. And having to hold it in for so long. Nikau is lucky to have you, Pania. You're always looking out for him."

"I try," she said softly.

"How about we give him a day to remember tomorrow? We'll make it lighthearted and freaking exciting. He'll feel such a sense of achievement after snowboarding that glacier, don't you think? Maybe then he'll start to believe in himself. He's not a bad egg Pania — he just needs to see his potential."

Pania grinned. She had put her gloves back on, and held one up for a padded high five.

Then Jabu got reflective. He wondered whether he should share his thoughts. Family business was such a personal thing. But still, he wanted to help Pania and Nikau to open up. After a long pause, he spoke. "The only thing is… family secrets lead to mistrust. How about you tell him the truth about his Dad? Talk to him about what you've shared with me. Get it all out in the open."

As he spoke, he saw a cloud veil over her eyes. He knew that he had overstepped the mark. She stared out at the distant view, breaking eye contact. The moment of close sharing was over.

"Nope, that's not happening," she said. "It would be a betrayal to Ma." Her next comment cut him. "Don't meddle." Her tone was as icy as the 'stalactites' that hung from the cafe door.

"Okay. Sorry." He zipped his mouth closed with a single gesture, his lips tightening in a straight line.

After the last sip of cold coffee, Jabu and Pania skied down the mountain to find the others. Jabu considered the weightiness of their family story. He had wanted to comfort Pania, but she had shut him out. After sharing so much, she had retreated into a shell, and he couldn't reach her there. As an orphan, he knew immeasurable loss, but he had never become detached. He allowed himself to feel and felt everything deeply. Her rebuttal stung like the windblown snowflakes on his skin. He tried to catch up with Pania, but she skied so fast down the slopes that he could not see her. Perhaps she wanted to put the moment of emotional intimacy behind her. Girls were so confusing!

The man on the ski lift was forgotten as Jabu thought only of Pania. He felt harnessed to the highs and lows of their interactions. Happy when she smiled at him, downcast when she removed her gaze. He was losing his sense of self. He found her combination of strength and vulnerability endearing. And, as the magnetic mountain lured them to greater heights, he felt powerless but to follow her up, up, up to the glacier.

17

THE QUEST

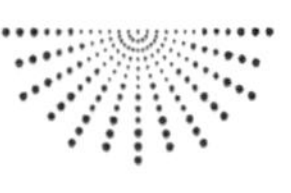

NIKAU

It was another bluebird day. With a brazen blue sky, and the forecast clear, the group set up the mountain feeling as if nothing could go wrong. The Prussian-blue heavens foregrounded the brilliant white mountain in breathtaking contrast. To Nikau's relief, Pania had agreed that today was a good day to ski and snowboard down the Mangaturuturu glacier. So here they were — Nikau, Pania, Jabu and Kyle, on the High Noon ski lift.

"We need to stick together and be sensible," said Pania in an annoyingly bossy tone.

"Did you know you can't outrun a lahar?" interrupted Nikau, "So if there happens to be a volcanic eruption, make sure you're not in a valley," He thought he would scare the South African visitors for a laugh.

Jabu's big brown eyes widened. Kyle shrugged nonchalantly, not relinquishing his chilled surfer image.

"Don't worry guys, slim chance of that," said Pania.

Eight legs hung over the edge of the ski chair. Three sets of skis, and one snowboard, hovered, awaiting action. Ice cold air brushed

90

against their faces, adding to the thrill of being suspended, high above the recreational skiers below. Ruapehu was invigorating. Nikau felt alert, alive, and momentarily forgot his worries.

From the top of the High Noon lift, they skied and snowboarded along the Solitude trail. They made their way around the perimeter of the mountain and crossed the upper slopes of various runs. Skiers raced down the trails like they were practising for the Winter Games. The group had to time their crossing with precision. It was like sprinting across a double highway. Keeping their altitude high was especially hard on the thigh muscles that burned and shook with exertion.

After they had crossed the furthest run in the Turoa Ski Fields, Pania stopped. Below them was a bowl. Up in the distance, a saddle ridge.

"Pare's Saddle," said Pania breathlessly. She had pulled out Papa Joe's map to check her bearings. "This is where we put on our climbing skins."

Nikau unclipped his snowboard and attached it to his backpack. The others attached skins to their skis.

"This is the hardest part. Once we reach the top of the saddle, it will be worth the climb. You'll see," said Pania. She had a goofy grin on her face.

"We get it, you're in your element," said Nikau sarcastically.

Jabu shot him a look of disapproval. Since when was Jabu her protector? Then, without another word, Pania started climbing. Soon the three skiers had gained significant ground while Nikau lagged behind. Climbing with snowboots was tough going. But he knew it would be worth every step. He imagined the exquisite perfection of snowboarding down the glacier. Putting one heavy foot in front of the other, he trudged on. It was hot and tiring, and he began to sweat in his thermals. The steeper the climb, the more he fell behind.

"Hurry up slow coach," shouted Pania.

She would be congratulating herself on the ease of skins, and feeling frustrated at his slow progress.

In pride, Nikau shouted back, "Go on ahead, I'll catch up."

After a while, the gap was too large for him to be able to hear Pania, but she continually stopped and turned back, waving at him. He gave a thumbs up for them to continue, although he low key wished they would slow down for him.

The distance between them grew, and even though they turned back to check on him, they did not stop. He sneezed as he looked up the mountain into the bright sun at their diminishing silhouettes.

Frustrated, Nikau stopped. He slumped down on a snowy ridge on the slope. Cool water soothed his parched throat as he sipped from a water bottle. He applied lip balm and admired the view before a low passing cloud obscured the scenery. For a few minutes, the visibility was so poor that he could barely see his hand in front of his face. He decided to wait for it to clear. The wind had picked up, bringing the cloud, but it would be likely to blow over as soon as it had come.

It felt slightly unnerving, sitting on a steep slope in the blinding mist. Like someone had tied a white bandage around his open eyes. Moving now would be careless. The fog swirled around him with shimmies of snow. *The weather better not turn nasty*, he thought with a shiver. Still, at least he was far, far away from Axel. He almost wanted to laugh out loud, thinking of his Dad, sitting at that cafe in Ohakune, waiting for him. *I'm a fox*, he thought. He grinned.

When the cloud finally cleared, Nikau realised he was not alone. A solo skier was skinning his way up the steep slope towards him, only a few feet away now. He had appeared out of nowhere, like a Yetti. Nikau recognised the camo pants. Axel!

Nikau shouted down to his Dad, trying to act casual. "Are you following me again?" He felt more like prey than fox now.

"How about 'Hello Dad'," said Axel between laboured breaths. Nikau froze, unsure of how to react.

Axel soon reached him and sat down beside him.

Before Nikau could say another word, Axel began a lecture.

"You lied to me again, you little runt. You promised you'd meet me in the village today, didn't you? You guaranteed you would meet me at the cafe and tell me where my stash is. Yet, once again, you tried to slip away."

Nikau said nothing.

"Did you think for one moment that I'd give up?"

"No, Sir," lied Nikau.

"Now listen to me. You need to quit this game and come back with me now. You can't outrun me, son."

"But the others will see I'm missing and…"

"They won't notice until they get to the top and stop to look back. By that time we'll be halfway to Auckland." This was delivered dead-pan. Nikau couldn't tell if Axel was either exceptionally patient or simmering.

"Why would I come with you?"

"Well, first of all, I need a fix. And when I need a fix, I get nasty. But that aside, think of the spoils, boy. That stash is worth a fortune. I'll make sure your pockets are well lined for delivering the goods to me. Also, I assume Vito has been arrested for stealing that Mustang, so all the more for you." Axel patted him on the back, his voice oily. Nikau realised his father was trying a new tactic. Nikau had foiled Axel a few times, and now the man was trying to grease him up.

"I'm not a crim," replied Nikau curtly.

"Oh but you are son, you've got yourself embroiled in this, and the only way out is to cooperate with me."

Nikau looked up the mountain at the shadowy figures, climbing, further and further away. How would he catch up with them? And what if Axel followed him and told Pania about the stash? She would be so disappointed in him. *I have to keep her out of this*, he thought. He had to lose Axel, somehow. To make matters worse, he was busting for a pee.

"Give me a moment," he said, buying time.

Feeling cornered, Nikau was not thinking straight when he unstrapped his snowboard and placed it beside him. He turned to face the mountain and urinated, watching the yellow pee make a hole in the snow as he tried to work out his next move.

"Your board!" yelled Axel.

Nikau looked over his shoulder to see his board, sliding down the long slope into the bowl that runs parallel to the glacial valley. It bounded over rocks and managed not to flip over, but made a beeline for lower gravity. It blazed a trail down into the bowl as if ridden by a superior ghost boarder.

Nikau was dumbstruck.

"You idiot!" said Axel.

Nikau said nothing, staring as if into an abyss.

"Always keep one foot strapped in, or place your board upside down on the bindings, don't you know that?"

"I wasn't thinking," Nikau grumbled. He felt like a toddler, getting a reprimand.

"Yeah, like when you hid my stash. You seem to have a problem with that. Head in the clouds boy."

The board had settled on a lump of snow at the far side of the bowl. It had slowed down as the bowl curved upwards, and friction had overcome gravity.

"Ah, stink!" said Nikau.

"Well at least it didn't turn down the mountain, else it would have gone like a kid in a water-slide chute. Pfffffft, gone."

"You're not helping."

Nikau stared down at his board, fuming, and crossing his arms against his chest.

"Son", said Axel, softening. He sounded almost kind, like the idea of the father he had missed out on as a boy. He really needed a Dad right now. Axel patted Nikau on the back.

"It's not a big deal, I'll make my way down there with you. It's not a good idea to be on the mountain alone. Then we can figure out what to do."

They began to make their way down the slope into the bowl.

"We can start a business together…" said Axel.

"I don't want to do drug-dealing Dad! I've been thinking about my future lately. I love this mountain so much. I want to train to become a snowboard instructor, and learn to drive a snowplough and come and work here." He felt excited at the idea, and it took shape as he spoke about it. "Then I can get into the marketing side and…" He didn't know why he was sharing this with a man who had lost his trust.

"Hey," said Axel with a smarmy grin. "With the money from the stash, we could buy shares in the winter sports business. But first, we need buyers. You'll have to help me sell the stash to your friends and schoolmates."

The words hit Nikau like a splash of cold water during an afternoon snooze.

My friends. He wants me to sell to my own friends. Just like he sold his friend Vito to the cops.

They walked in silence, sinking deep into the soft snow, their footprints leaving a trail of elongated holes behind them. Nikau thought about damaged lives. About addicts, and about his classmate who had developed drug-induced schizophrenia. The boy had hung himself. He had seen so many kids' lives, ruined. Parties and car accidents. Alcohol, weed, hard drugs. They all came with a price. Yet that was his playground. *No more!*

Walking in the pure white snow, he felt strengthened by the ancient mountain. He made up his mind. Nikau did not want that stuff getting out on the streets. *It's probably long gone, but if I find it in the bin, I'll destroy it when I get back to Auckland,* he resolved.

Finally, they reached the snowboard in silence. Nikau looked up at Pare Saddle, squinting into the white glare. Three small figures, like ants, stood on the upper, mountainside, above the saddle, looking out —presumably looking for him.

He had a glacier yet to snowboard, a quest to finish and his Dad was a thorn in his side.

"So, you in?" asked Axel, seeming uncomfortable with Nikau's silence.

"No, I won't do it," said Nikau firmly.

"Do what?"

"No. I won't sell it to my friends, or to anyone else. I'm not giving it to you." He dared not tell Axel he had thrown the stuff away. "I'm going to climb back up to Pania and ride this glacier. This is where we say goodbye. Don't contact me again."

Axel's face turned violently angry in an instant.

"You don't seem to understand," said Axel, picking up Nikau's snowboard and turning back the way they came. "You either come with me now, or you'll have to walk off this mountain. And it's a long way on foot."

Axel trudged off slowly through the deep snow with Nikau's mode of transport tucked under his armpit. Nikau felt his temper boil over. Then, as if he had summoned it himself, the mountain shuddered like a mini earthquake and began to erupt.

18

RUAPEHU SPEAKS

NIKAU

23 SEPTEMBER 1995

The ground shook. The mountain spoke. Thermally heated steam and gas exploded through the crater lake. Black jets of ash, sediment and water speared the sky like crystal shards, growing instantly. Cauliflower shaped clouds of ash and steam spread upwards and expanded outward. White arcs rocketed high into the air, and torpedo rocks succumbed to gravity and began to pummel the snowy mountain.

A rock bomb landed on the summit face, displacing a thick layer of unstable snow. Nikau watched in horror as an avalanche slid down the slope towards Pania, Jabu and Kyle. Nothing would stop the momentum of the wall of snow. Their ant-sized bodies were swallowed by the deluge that slid down into the dip of Pare Saddle.

Nikau thinned his eyes at the sun, but he could not see them. They had disappeared into the mouth of the avalanche. The mountain continued to belch out missiles and ash clouds that towered miles above the summit. Nikau bounded over to Axel.

"Come, help me! We've got to save Pania!" he urged.

"No, you come with me, boy — let's get ourselves to safety," said Axel.

"But what about Pania? Your daughter?" Nikau was screaming the words. His voice sounded hysterical, even to himself.

Axel grabbed hold of Nikau's jacket and tried to run, tugging Nikau with him, senselessly down towards the bowl. *But lahars flow into valleys!*

Nikau punched his father in the chin, ducking as Axel tried to return the insult. Their eyes met. The face of the man who clung to his ski jacket looked so familiar to him, yet it distorted with monstrous rage and fear. Known and yet incomprehensible. It was not the face he had conjured up for all those years, of someone fatherly. Axel held fast as Nikau tried to turn towards the avalanche that had engulfed his sister.

A rock bomb exploded through the air, trailing a white path and pounded into the snow a few yards from them.

Then, as if inevitable, the crater lake wall broke. A river of black sludge surged down the mountain, finding the valley and gushing towards them at ninety miles an hour. The deadly flow would sweep over them in moments. Axel released Nikau's arm and began to plough up the slope of the bowl, out of the valley. He tripped and fell face-first into the powder in his haste, dropping Nikau's snowboard.

Nikau could only think of Pania.

My sister. I have to get to her. Our father doesn't even care.

Nikau snatched his snowboard, leaving the man crawling through the snow in a frenzy of fear. The lahar was almost upon them now. He would be safe, but Axel was directly in the lahar's path.

In a moment of mercy, Nikau turned back, to help get Axel out of harm's way. His steps felt laboured — as if time had slowed down for him and sped up for the lahar, which was an inky stretch away. He would not get back to Axel in time. He held his breath.

The black wall of volcanic mudflow raced past, coldly oblivious to the human life it almost devoured. It had streaked a path down the centre of the valley, a yard from Axel. The black river continued on, carrying rocks and debris to the Mangaturuturu river. An ugly stain on the virgin white snow, like spilt ink on a page.

Nikau decided to leave Axel to his own destiny and climbed hastily out of the valley. Axel shouted after him. His voice was muffled by the sound of the mountain, belching and coughing. He did not turn around to see if Axel was following him. Compelled by his love for his sister, he chased up the slope.

At the top of the western slope of the bowl-shaped valley, he reached the edge of the Mangaturuturu glacier. It was thinly coated in ash. The snow thinned out for a section, and he moved swiftly. He hoped he was gaining ground between him and Axel. Or maybe Axel would go the other way, off the mountain, running from danger like a coward.

Adrenalin fuelled him. Nikau moved with the strength of youth. He paused at the bottom of a steep slope that would need to be climbed to get to the base of the avalanche. Without a pick or climbing boots, it would be treacherous.

Nikau attached his snowboard to his backpack and began to climb. He knew he couldn't look back, he couldn't look down, but he faced the white wall and made his way up, one boot at a time. If he lost his grip now, he could slide all the way into the barrelling lahar in the valley below. He was gripped with a fear of falling. But he had to get to Pania.

Finally, the slope eased into a gentle gradient, then flattened out. Nikau lay cheek down on the snow, arms spread out. He was panting. *Don't stop now.* He willed himself to get up and keep going, but first, he looked back, just once to see if Axel was following him. There was no trace of the man. Perhaps he was trying to get down the mountain. Only, Axel wouldn't be able to cross the lahar to get back to the ski lifts, so he would have to stay on this side of the mountain and make his way down to the forests.

Then Nikau turned back towards the terrors that lay ahead. A mushroom of cloud was expanding towards him. Soon he would have no visibility. Rocks continued to spew out of the crater and barrel into the snow. If one landed on him, he wouldn't live to tell anyone about it. Twenty metres ahead of him stood the edge of the avalanche. A wall of snow. He approached it with dread. Where would he begin to dig for Pania?

Nikau started digging randomly. Occasional bombs fell near him, and showers of ash coated his ski jacket. He dug in one area, then moved on and tried another, all the while thinking that she, they, would not have been able to hold their breath all this time. But he would not give up. Tears turned to ice on his cheeks, pooling in his goggles and forming a crusty layer. The cold bit into him with metal teeth. His sweat had turned to ice on his skin, and his shivering became a constant tremor. He scrambled and dug, like a dog on a beach, digging one hole, then another. There seemed to be no order to his digging, only frantic desperation. Finally, he collapsed to his knees and wept.

Nikau cried bitter tears until he was spent. Then he stood up and waved a fist at the mountain.

"Give her back!" he yelled with all the breath in his lungs.

The echo of his voice pierced into his very soul. The impassive mountain ignored him. Unmoved, Ruapehu continued to erupt giant clouds of ash. The white, black and grey clouds seemed to stretch miles high. A helicopter circumnavigated the mountain, keeping a safe distance from the ash. Nikau screamed and waved his hands. The helicopter circled a few times, then flew away.

Nikau turned his back on the avalanche and the raging mountain. He collapsed to his knees and stared at the wide glacial valley stretching out below the ridge. He had seen postcards of Fox Glacier and Franz Josef. This glacier was unlike the thick, slow crawling slugs of ice he had imagined. He had wondered how Pania had thought they could ski on a glacier of ice. The Mangaturuturu glacial valley, wide and covered in untouched snow, originated at the summit of the mountain, near the crater, and ended in a river far below. Her white veil was tainted with ash, and an inky black tear ran down, down to the river far below him.

How wonderful it would have been to ski and board down there with his sister.

"Oh Pania, I don't know what to do", he said weakly.

In the very fibre of his bones, Nikau could not believe Pania was dead. He felt as if she was still there, on the mountain somewhere. *Don't stay, it's not safe*, he heard playing through his mind, in her voice.

His eyes scanned the mountain to work out the best way down. *What would Pania have done? If she had made it. What would she want me to do?*

He plotted his route. He would have to climb down the steep snow-coated ridge he had ascended. Usually, that would be an epic slope to board down, but if he gained too much speed, he would end up in the lahar. *Tickets. I'm too young to cark it*, he thought.

Nikau figured that once he made it to the gentle valley, he would be wedged between the lahar on the left and a steep, rocky ridge to the right. He would have to snowboard in an almost straight line parallel to the lahar. The route was a metre wide, even narrower in places. He hoped it would lead to the forest. At least the trees would offer some shelter and distance from the bombs and ash. If he could make it to the woods, he would also be closer to the mountain circumference road, and to help.

"I'm sorry, Pania," he cried out. "I know you would want me to keep going. You wouldn't want me to die here." His teeth chattered. *I have to keep going, else I'll freeze to death, or get flattened. I have to hold on to hope. That you got out, somehow... That I can too.*

19

A SONG IN THE FOREST

NIKAU

After losing his foothold and sliding down the last ten feet of a steep decline, it was a relief to be back on his snowboard again. Nikau threaded his way between lahar and cliff. His body ached from the fall, but nothing seemed broken. The narrow pathway of snow between barrelling lahar and steep cliffs became narrower still, like a funnel. He hoped he would not run out of a strip of snow to board on. At least on the snowboard, he could make speedy progress away from the belching volcano. He had supreme control of his board. A slight shift of weight on his feet could steer him. He veered around small rocks, avoiding sharp edges that jutted out from the cliff on his right and the twisting lahar on his left. It astounded him, that though he was snowboarding like a maniac, compared to the lahar, it seemed as if he was going backwards. As the path narrowed, Nikau considered his options. He was not a confident climber. The rocky face on his right looked impossible to scale. He hoped he would not become hemmed in by the lahar.

Missiles rained down on the mountain, some rocks, some enormous boulders. Nikau bent his knees and leant forward to pick up

102

speed, fear catching in his throat. Most of the ash had blown sky high when the mountain erupted, but now it fell in a descending veil of grey. He coughed and pulled his neck warmer up over his face with one hand.

Curiously, he reached a section on the pathway where it appeared as if other skiers had travelled. It was difficult to make out the number of tracks, or even if they were ski tracks to be sure. The veneer of ash made it hard to decipher. A quiet voice of hope suggested to him that they may belong to Pania, but, a taunting inner voice told him the tracks belonged to Axel.

Up ahead, the pathway disappeared, replaced by the sky. Nikau's heart quickened as he realised a sheer drop lurked only a few seconds ahead of him. He braked, careful not to slide into the inky force on his left. He slid to a halt, coming to a stop only a few feet before the cliff. Beyond him, a view of the forest stretched out endlessly. He peered over the edge of a steep wall of rock. The lahar fell over the cliff like a waterfall of sludge. He had no choice but to clip his board on his backpack again, and rock climb down the face as far from the waterfall as possible. The vast glacier had converged into a narrow river valley, fenced in by rocky cliffs on each side.

With immense concentration, Nikau lowered himself, one foot and handhold at a time. This time he did not fall but reached the bottom in a fearful sweat. At the base of the waterfall, his eyes followed the river valley to a swing bridge. He skipped towards it across a flatbed of rock. At the bridge, Nikau hesitated. The route off the mountain looked easier on the other side of the bridge, though he couldn't be sure.

In two minds, he took a tentative first step onto the wooden swing bridge. The lahar was running only a few feet below. The bridge swayed as he mounted it. He hoped the Department of Conservation had maintained the ropes and wooden rungs. Looking up towards the mountain for possible debris, Nikau sighted a boulder, sliding towards him at speed like a mini mountain. He instinctively jumped backwards off the bridge. The rock smashed through the wooden slats, making light work of the wood and rope, dragging it like a fishing net.

Nikau retreated, his heart pounding in his throat. He had no choice but to continue towards the forest. He was well and truly cut off. Dejected, he walked across a plate of rock, where hardy red tussock and lichen grew. After half an hour, he came across a pond sized lake. He had heard of this lake, described by trampers as Lake Surprise. It was not reflective but muted. He staggered towards it, knelt down, removed his gloves and cupped his hands in the water to drink. Then he noticed the thick layer of ash. It was possibly toxic. Nikau removed his neck warmer and used it as a sieve to strain the water into his empty drinking bottle. He had a long, thirsty drink of the smoky flavoured water. *Not bad*, he thought. He filled his bottle again. *Thank you*, he thought, looking skyward.

Feeling refreshed, Nikau walked around the rim of the lake and headed away from the mountain. Soon he would have no choice but to enter the forest. He turned back for a last look at angry Ruapehu. Caught between a furnace and a deep dark wood. *Great options*, he thought bitterly.

He knew he should press on, but he stood still, staring mournfully back up at the place where the mountain had swallowed his sister.

Then, shaking him into action, another volcanic bomb seared through the air and splashed into the lake, sizzling and sending out ripples. Water splashed over the rim of the lake. Without delay, Nikau dashed to the podocarp forest beyond. At the perimeter, he pushed aside the frond of a palm and entered the woods.

The forest was almost impenetrable. Nikau used his snowboard to hack his way through ferns and undergrowth. Inside the forest, it was dank and eerie, almost devoid of light. He startled at a fantail that flitted around his head bossily. At least the bird made him feel less alone.

"Hello little fella," he said, surprised at his croaky voice. "I won't disturb your nest."

On he trudged, wondering how to figure out which way was South West. By his reckoning, that was the direction that would lead towards the main road that circumnavigated the mountain. He hoped he might happen upon a well-worn tramping path.

The light dimmed, and it seemed he was lost. His situation appeared helpless. *What a fool*, he thought. He sat down in the humus and rested his head in his hands. He needed to think. He wanted to cry. To weep for his sister, and for himself. But tears did not come easily for Nikau. Instead, his heart sobbed, and his eyes remained dry. He looked up at the dappled sunlight. He tried to use the hour hand on his watch and the position of the sun, but he couldn't remember how that worked. Another science lesson he had mucked around in. A useful lesson not learnt. He got up and pressed on, directionless.

After an hour of tireless hacking through dense forest, Nikau heard singing. It was a beautiful harmony. A female voice led, while one or two male baritones hummed as if they didn't know the words. It sounded like Pania! And Jabu and Kyle. Were they ghosts of the forest? Angels? Forest nymphs that would lead him into graver danger? Or his sister, alive? His feet took charge and ran towards the sweet sound.

"Wairua Tapu, Kuhu Mai,

Nau mai ki konei

Wairua Tapu, Arahia,

Korero mai ano…"

It was a song about the Holy Spirit they used to sing at his Ma's church before she withdrew into herself. As the voices lifted in praise, welcoming God into their presence, Nikau ran. Faster, closer, towards the angelic voices. The glow of a fire drew him nearer. And then he was upon them.

Pania, Jabu and Kyle sat around a modest fire. Their eyes were closed as they sang and praised God. How could they be praising God when Nikau was lost to them? But then his resistance crumbled, and he too began to praise God inwardly and thank Him, that he had found his sister, alive.

"Pania," he said gruffly, the stubborn tears starting to flow. She opened her eyes and her face filled with surprise, then joy. Pania leapt up and ran to him, holding him tight. They both cried and shuddered.

"We'd been praying for you, pleading… that you'd get away from the eruption safely! We searched for you, but it got too dangerous to stay up there, and we had to flee. Oh, Nikau!" She squeezed him again. "Why did you fall behind? Probably a good thing you did. I guess you weren't taken by the avalanche?"

"Nope," he said, trying to figure out how to best answer her. He decided not to ruin the reunion by telling her about Axel and the whole sordid business about the stash. Nor would he tell her how Axel wouldn't even help him look for his own daughter in the avalanche. It was all too awful. A secret he must keep. He lowered himself onto a leafy patch in front of the modest fire. "I climbed up, and couldn't find you…" he said, swallowing back a lump. "I knew I had to get out of there, so I boarded like a boss to get away from those missiles. Do you think we're out of range?"

"Hope so, but who knows," said Pania, her eyes wide with fear.

"How did you survive the avalanche?" Nikau asked, as they all sat around the fire, sharing stories.

"Kyle and I managed to ski like bullets to the right of it and out of danger," said Jabu. "But when we looked back, Pania was not behind us."

"I had been swallowed whole," said Pania, shivering at the memory.

"I made a fist in front of my face as I tumbled, knowing I would need an air pocket."

"How did you know that?" asked Nikau.

Pania sat quietly, staring ahead. "I saw it on a documentary once," she replied finally. She was clearly in shock. He would have to coax the story gently.

Nikau added another branch to the fire. "Then what happened, sis?"

She took a deep breath. "When I stopped sliding with the snow, I pushed outward with my fist. The snow gave a couple of inches, leaving enough room to give me air to breathe for a few minutes. I tried to stay calm and slow my breathing."

"Far out," said Nikau slowly. He was impressed with his sister's strength of mind.

"I spat into the small pocket. That way, I knew I wasn't upside down."

"Yuck," said Nikau, chuckling. The relief that she was alive had made him jubilant. "So then did you try to dig yourself out?"

"I couldn't dig. My arms were pinned to my sides," she said, staring into the fire.

"Sheez, Pania, you must've been bricking it."

"I thought I would suffocate, to be honest," she said quietly. "I remember thinking, 'is this really how I am going to die?'"

"We raced over to the base of the avalanche," added Kyle gallantly. "To the area where we had seen Pania being taken and started to dig with our skis."

"And we managed to dig her out!" said Jabu, smiling triumphantly.

"Legends!" said Nikau. "Bloody legends."

For the moment, there was peace in the camp. They had a long night ahead of them and were miles from any track or road, but for now, they were alive and together. Nikau sat next to Pania, feeling like he never wanted to leave her side again. He'd be her guard. Her brother.

"I'll get you out of here, sis," he said.

She smiled with her eyes and nodded.

A pensive silence spread out as the fire sputtered through damp kindling while volcanic ash drifted down between the leaves.

PANIA'S PEPEHA

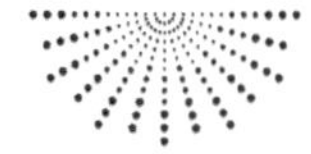

Ko Tongariro te maunga
Ko Taupō te moana
Ko Tūwharetoa te iwi
Ko Te Heuheu te tangata
I am Pania!

Tongariro is the mountain
    Taupō is the great inland sea
    Tūwharetoa are the people
    Te Heuheu is the man
    I am Pania!

RUSTY THE RECLUSE

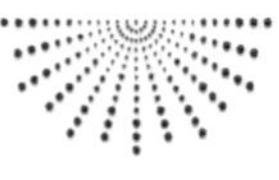

PANIA

Pania sat beside Jabu on the damp undergrowth, watching her brother as he cut ferns with his penknife and snapped branches to make a bivouac. Kyle offered to help. She leaned on Jabu's shoulder. Jabu seemed reluctant to move and shyly put his arm around her. She tucked her head into his armpit and listened to his slow and rhythmic heartbeat. He smelt like ash and snow.

"Shout if you need a hand?" said Jabu halfheartedly.

"No, sit with me, please," whispered Pania. After almost suffocating in an avalanche, and praying her brother wasn't lost to them, or dead, Pania needed Jabu's presence. He grounded her. She wanted him close.

"Na, we're all good mate, thanks," said Nikau, clearly concentrating on the job at hand.

Pania thought about how capable her brother was, yet he didn't know it. He was bright, innovative and brave, yet he didn't believe it. She watched him stacking up branches on the bivouac.

"Where did you learn to make a shelter like this?" she asked.

"Ah, we did it at Camp Kawau. Didn't you learn how to make bivouacs at camp?"

"Na mate, I probably chose kayaking that day. We couldn't do everything the year we went."

"True, you were in a big group that year," he said, adding a palm frond to the shelter.

Then Pania's thoughts turned to the dryness in her throat.

"Does anyone have water?" asked Pania.

"I do," said Nikau. "It's from Lake Surprise."

"Did you drink that? You'll get Guardia if you don't boil it first," said Pania, pulling a face.

"Oops, too late," said Nikau, shrugging. "I drank a whole bottle full and then refilled it. Better than dying of dehydration."

"I guess," said Pania. She felt parched.

Nikau put down a branch and fished his water bottle from his backpack, bringing it over to her. She took a couple of small, grateful sips. "Can I share it around?"

"Sure, just leave me some…" he said.

Jabu and Kyle took a long sip each. The water in Nikau's bottle was all they had between them.

"We'll have to make it last a few days — weeks even if we can't find our way out," said Pania.

The young men nodded. Jabu squeezed Pania closer, while the others finished the bivouac. Once completed, it was wide enough for them to all sleep under, side by side.

"We should try to get some shut-eye," said Kyle, climbing in and laying down. Jabu and Pania lay beside one another.

"I'm sleeping between you two!" said Nikau, budging his way in as they nestled down on the bed of leaves.

Neither of them objected.

"We'll need our sleep. Tomorrow might be a long day," whispered Pania.

"Yeah, night," said Nikau.

"Sweet dreams," said Jabu.

Kyle was already asleep.

Pania lay still, listening to the sounds of the forest at night, taking comfort in their togetherness and the sharing of body warmth.

For once Pania didn't mind her brother laying beside her with his careless elbows, his snoring and twitching. She propped herself up on her side and looked across at him. He was alive. That in itself was worth thanks and gratitude. She smiled as she watched him sleep. It was the only time he almost looked angelic.

Then she let her eyes wander across to Jabu, her sleeping African prince, his long black eyelashes curling and flickering, his lips full. Kissable. Her reliable friend Kyle lay at the opposite end of the bivouac, his back turned on them, and beanie pulled down. A few strands of blond hair spiked out from under the beanie. He hunched over, warding off the cold.

I got them all into this mess, she thought, *I hope I can get them out of it.*

Then she closed her eyes and surrendered to an exhausted but restless sleep.

In the morning they got moving early. They all agreed that the road to Ohakune was South West of the mountain, but they could not see Ruapehu through the dense canopy of trees. A thick ash cloud muted the sunlight. A sundial would not be possible.

"Let's follow the downward gradient of the slope," suggested Nikau.

"That could be misleading. It may take us down into a river valley," argued Kyle.

"No matter if it does," said Jabu, "at least then we'd have water."

"True dat," said Nikau.

They made steady progress as the morning rolled into midday.

"I'm hungry," Nikau grumbled. Pania wished he hadn't voiced it. He was the first to admit what they were all feeling. By putting words to his hunger, it became her most prominent thought.

"I could kill a burger," he added.

"Shutup would ya?" snapped Pania. "Let's stop for a sip of water."

"But seriously, what will we eat if we don't get out of this forest soon?"

"Don't you remember what Nana taught us? We could make a *Hīnaki* to trap eels in the river."

"Or a bow and arrow to shoot down some plump kererū," added Nikau.

"If we had to, I guess. And we could eat grasses and berries," she added.

"And trap rainwater," he said.

"Or drink river water, if we can find a river," she added.

"Looks like we chose the right people to be lost with," said Jabu to Kyle. "But let's hope it doesn't come to any of that."

And so they walked and talked, sometimes amiable, other times argumentative, always thirsty and hungry. Then, as the light faded and Nikau grumbled about having to build another bivouac, they came across an unexpected find.

In a grassy clearing, cobbled together with wood and tin, was a hut. A tiny window peered from walls made of old wooden cladding, that held up a rusted tin roof. Smoke rose steadily from a chimney at one end of the hut. At the other end stood a tank for collecting rainwater. In the distance, under a kauri tree was a dunny, painted bright blue.

Lured by the hope of help, food and shelter, they approached the hut. The door was closed, perhaps to keep the warmth in.

Jabu knocked.

There was no reply.

He knocked again, answered by more silence. Then he tentatively opened the door and entered. Pania crept into the dark space behind him, followed by Nikau and Kyle. At first, her eyes had to adjust to the dim light inside. It faded in through the window in grey shafts. A kitchen knife lay beside a cutting board on a makeshift bench. Unwashed pots and utensils teetered in the sink. Possum tails and skins hung from a wire line, suspended along the length of the hut.

A dead possum sprawled out on a table, half skinned. A bloody hunting knife lay unwashed beside it. It unnerved her. A bookshelf leaned incongruently against the opposite wall, beside a worn armchair. On the chair, a book lay open. A fire blazed in a wood burner on the far wall, upon which a pot simmered. Despite herself, Pania salivated at the aroma of a meaty stew, that hinted at forest onions and game.

"Anyone here?" she asked, although it was evident they were alone.

Before they could decide whether it was safe to stay, or prudent to clear out as fast as their legs could carry them, the door swung open.

"Who in Forest's name are you?" growled the voice of a red-bearded man, pointing a rifle in their faces.

They all spoke at once, explaining who they were and how they had escaped an avalanche and an eruption.

"We didn't mean to trespass," said Pania, fixing him with her most apologetic gaze. "We're lost in the forest and we're looking for shelter."

"We knocked," added Jabu.

"And then ya decided ta just let y'selves in eh?"

They nodded. "Sorry, mate," said Nikau.

"Ya just made y'selves at home," he said, placing his rifle down beside the doorway. "What else is this mountain going ta spew out?" he asked himself, shaking his head.

Pania couldn't help but stare at the man. She looked at his feet, wrapped in flax sandals, his blood-stained jeans and possum-fur waistcoat. She avoided eye contact but observed a silver-tipped ginger beard, ears that sprouted furry tufts and a shock of greying copper hair.

"I'm Rusty," he offered, putting out a blood-stained hand to shake.

It seemed rude not to shake his hand, which they did in turns.

"I'll expect yer all hungry, eh?" he asked, heading over to the pot, lifting the lid and giving it a stir.

"No, no, we're good," said Jabu. Pania wished he hadn't said that.

"Ah, well don't mind if I do," he said, walking over to the makeshift kitchen and pulling a ceramic bowl from a cupboard. He served himself a bowl of meaty stew, placed his book face down on the floor so as not to lose his place, and sunk into his armchair.

"Hungry work, huntin'," he said, before tucking into the stew.

Watching him eat was agonising. It smelt so good, yet he looked disgusting. Not a mouthful of stew made it from his spoon to his mouth without him spilling drops onto his beard. Bits of green plants stuck to his beard as he chewed.

"On second thoughts," said Nikau, "what's in it?"

"Don't be rude," whispered Pania.

"Ah, it's my infamous possum stew," he said, "cooked in secret forest 'erbs and freshly trapped rainwater."

"If you're offering, I might try some," ventured Nikau.

"You eat lad, you're gonna need it. Still a long way to walk to get outa these woods. Grab y'self a bowl 'n spoon or fork or whatever ya can find."

Nikau helped himself to a ladle of stew. There were no chairs, besides the one Rusty sat in. Nikau crossed his legs on the wooden floor by the fire and braved a spoonful.

Pania was aghast. This was Nikau the fussy eater, who had to have his meat and veg separate at home. Ma always joked and called him a "Food Separatist". Here he was chewing on a mouthful of possum and bitter greens. He tried to conceal the turning up of his cheek and flaring nostrils, munching and swallowing. They all watched. Then he took a bigger spoonful and shoved it in.

"Mmm, good," he said through a mouthful.

Encouraged, the others asked if they too could change their minds.

"I guess. I was hopin' it was gonna last me another day, but I can't have ya starvin' on me, can I?" Rusty grumbled. The red-haired recluse waved his hand towards the cupboard. Help y'selves. And after dinner, ya can boil some water and wash me dishes."

After serving themselves, the friends sat on the floor near the fire.

"Tough as old *takkies*," whispered Jabu. Pania had no idea what takkies were. Some South African word, she guessed. She suppressed a giggle because it sounded funny.

After they had eaten, Pania boiled water on the wood burner, and Jabu washed the dishes. Then Rusty invited them to sit with him near the fire.

"So how do you survive in the middle of the forest?" asked Kyle.

"Simple, laddie. I survive mostly on what the forest provides. But when I need a new book, or soap or dishwashing liquid, loo paper, that sorta thing, I go ta town."

"Town?"

"Yeah, I walk to Ohakune. Takes a few days. But I only do it twice a year or so. I sell my possum hides to the tourist shop and pick up some one dolla' books from the *sally*. A few supplies and then I'm off. I'm a recluse see. Hate people. Prefer me own company any day of the week…"

He did not make eye contact with them when he spoke but rolled his grey eyes upwards into the back of his eyelids. He frequently blinked, avoiding the windows to their souls. Denying them his.

"How do you know the way to Ohakune?" asked Kyle.

"I've got possum tails hammered into trees that lead ta the river. It's like an artery, see. Ya just follow the doodackie river, and it'll take ya to the Mangaturuturu river. Then it's easy. DOC has a tidy rope bridge and tramping tracks that lead ta town. Yer'l need water though. Fill up ya bottles. And ya can take one of me old pots ta boil the water in."

Pania had a feeling they were about to be turfed out. She did not want to face another cold night in the forest, so she thought about softening him with a gift. Her eyes scanned the room for ideas. His bookshelf housed J.R.R. Tolkien's "Lord of the Rings," trilogy, "The Bone People," by Keri Hulme and "The Haunting," by Margaret Mahy. She spotted "Once Were Warriors," by Alan Duff, "Whale Rider," by Witi Ihimaera and, to her surprise, the Bible. There were a few titles and authors she did not recognise, but on the whole, Pania was impressed with his library. The possum-hunting-recluse was a bibliophile. She knew exactly what to give him.

"Thank you for your kindness, Rusty," she said, pulling a dog eared copy of Maurice Gee's "The Halfmen of O" Trilogy from her backpack. Rusty's eyes gleamed. He snatched the book from her hands, settling back into his chair and starting to read without an acknowledgement.

"Anyone else got a book?" Pania whispered.

"I don't read," said Nikau.

"Me neither," Kyle agreed, giving Nikau a fist bump.

Jabu pulled a copy of "Cry the beloved country," from his backpack. Pania exchanged a look of affinity with him. He'd also brought a book on a ski trip! They were fellow bibliophiles.

"Give it to him as a *koha* later," she added in a low whisper.

Jabu gave her a thumbs up.

As Rusty read, and the fire blazed, the friends reclined on a sheepskin rug near the fire, propping their heads up on their backpacks.

"If we keep him distracted," whispered Pania, "we'll have a warm shelter for the night."

The others nodded, grinning.

They watched him as he turned page after page as if he had

forgotten he had rare visitors. Finally, his head nodded forward, and the book fell from his lap. Soon he was snoring like a lumberjack chopping wood. Nikau and Kyle were the next to drift into a slumber.

Jabu placed an ample log in the wood burner. Then, he lay down next to Pania. She turned to him and smiled. He leaned forward and kissed her on the lips, and she felt herself blushing. He wrapped his arms around her, and she fell asleep in his strong embrace.

2 2

A WARNING

PANIA

25 SEPTEMBER 1995

"What are ya all still doing here?" grumbled Rusty on waking. "Best be on ya way, I've got things ta do."

He silently built a new fire in the wood burner.

"Nothin' worse than an overstayer," he muttered under his breath.

Even so, he boiled a pot of water and made them each a mug of *kawakawa* tea.

"Good for ya circulation," he said. Then, his brow knitted. "Before ya go, I'd best be telling ya about the man in the woods."

"A man?" asked Pania. She noticed Nikau's eyes narrow.

"You'd better be careful out there," said Rusty gravely. "Don't be dawdlin' in the woods. Get out as quick as ya can."

Jabu chuckled. Pania elbowed him sharply.

"Strange. Ya don't see a soul in the forest in years, and then ya see city folk twice in one day." He scratched his head, perplexed.

"Who did you see?" asked Nikau, frowning.

Rusty looked out the window, into the thicket, fixing his mind's eye on the memory.

"He was skulking in the forest like he was on somethin's trail," he continued. "I've done enough huntin' ta know when someone is a hunter. The man looked up and saw the hut. I was standin' in the doorway. He stared me in the eyes for a moment." Rusty shivered. "Now don't get me wrong, I'm not insane, but I'm mad enough ta know when someone is a sarmie short of a picnic. His eyes … " Rusty drifted off.

"What happened next?" asked Kyle.

"Neither of us said a word. Then he took a step towards the shack. I went inside, got me rifle and took aim, ready ta shoot if he took a step closer. He fixed me with a cold stare. Pale eyes in deep, black eye sockets. Neither of us stirred. Like a mountain lion and a deer, the moment before one of 'em makes their move, we appraised each other. 'You're not welcome here,' is what I thought. He understood my wordless message. He turned away and slunk into the bush, looking defeated. Ta be honest, I've kept me rifle with me ever since. I wouldn't want ta come across the likes of him in the forest, day or night."

After the soliloquy, Rusty went to the bookshelf and pulled a flask from behind a book. He unscrewed the lid and took a long swig.

"Okay, well, thanks for the warning," said Pania, trying not to show her disbelief. "We'll be heading off now. Thank you so much for your hospitality."

Jabu handed Rusty his book. "Here you go, a little gift to say thanks."

Rusty's facial hair made way for a broad grin. He seemed to have forgotten his fearful encounter with a mad forest stalker. He opened the book and read the first sentence aloud, "There is a lovely road that runs from Ixopo into the hills. These hills are grass covered and rolling, and they are lovely beyond any singing of it." He nodded approvingly at Jabu. "Thank you, son. And I hope ya meet a lovely road on ya travels. Be safe fellas," he said, flicking his head to the door before settling back into his armchair to read.

Rusty did not seem to hear their thanks and goodbyes. He was engrossed in the first page of "Cry the Beloved Country", his flax covered feet stretched out in comfort.

And so, they began to follow the trail through the bush, marked out by possum-tails nailed to trees.

"What a nutcase," said Jabu. "I reckon that stalker dude was a total figment of his imagination. Probably the shadow of a tree, after too much whiskey."

"Whiskey, kawakawa tea, possum-stew and books — that's what he lives on," said Pania. "All alone in the forest, for heavens knows how many years. You've got to go a bit spare. Maybe the characters in his books become real in his head and begin to appear!"

Jabu and Kyle laughed, but Nikau was sullen. Pania had noticed that he had begun to startle at every unexpected rustle, mistaking misshaped trees for people.

"Bro, chill out," said Pania. "Do you believe in Hansel and Gretel? Rusty's story is a fairy tale dude… there is nobody in this forest but us, okay."

Nikau nodded.

"Our main adversaries are cold, thirst and hunger," said Kyle. "So let's pick up the pace."

They pressed on, soon giving up on the idea of finding further possum tails on trees. *Rusty has the forest mapped out in his mind,* thought Pania. He knew precisely where his possum trail markers were, but for them, it was like finding a breadcrumb on a beach.

As the day wore on, and they snaked through the dense woods, they were startled by the booming sound of the volcano, erupting again. The ground vibrated. A kererū swooped from a tree, wings wooshing audibly. The dense forest obscured Mt. Ruapehu from them which only made the rumbling and belching more unnerving. The air was acrid with a thick sulphurous odour. Pania pulled her neck warmer up over her nose and mouth. Ash fell sootily, coating the forest. They walked with more purpose, thinking of home, of fresh air and a hot meal.

Hours passed. No possum tails nailed to trees were to be found. No gurgling 'doodackie' river to point the way. They traipsed through an endless terrain of pre-Jurassic looking ferns and podocarps.

The fading light took them by surprise. Dusk was not much different to the dim ashen light of day.

"We'd better make a fire," suggested Nikau. "Here's a good spot to make a bivouac for the night."

They set to work, fractious and dejected. Soon they had a roaring fire, thanks to Kyle's lighter. Nikau and Kyle started building a shelter. When complete, they sat around the flames in exhausted silence, contemplating the long, hungry night ahead.

"Put the jug on would ya?" said Pania, handing Nikau the pot and her water bottle. "We'll go and pick some kawakawa leaves. That tea was good." She gestured to Jabu to join her.

"See if you can find us some edible berries," said Nikau, "But don't go far, okay…"

23

THE SYMBOL OF A PIKORUA

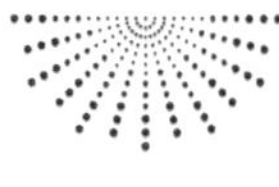

PANIA

Pania slipped her hand into Jabu's as they walked away from the others.

"You need to look for the leaves with the biggest holes. Those are the best tea-making leaves," she explained.

"Why so?" asked Jabu.

"They've got the caterpillar's approval," she said, not knowing the real reason.

He laughed. She loved his laugh, deep and bubbling, like a well of generosity.

They picked a handful of choice leaves, making sure not to wander too far as the grey dusk turned lavender. Jabu took hold of her hands, pulling her to face him. "What does your twisted greenstone necklace symbolise?" he asked.

"Have you been waiting to ask me that," she retorted, laughing.

His face crinkled in a smile.

"It is the bond between two people, whether connected by blood, or friendship, or…" she paused.

"Or?"

123

"Or love," she finished.

"Who gave it to you?" He asked.

"My Ma," she said. "I know we'll get out of here, and I'll see my Ma and Pa again, because the *pikorua* says that despite twists and turns, our lives will come together again."

"That's cool." He swallowed.

"Did you think it was from a boyfriend?" she asked, teasingly.

"Just checking," he said.

"Nope, I'm single," said Pania. She looked into his big brown eyes. They were like planets.

Then, she pressed her lips against his. He responded. For a moment, a gust of wind up high tugged a cloud of ash from the moon. In the silver light, they kissed. It was the coming together of two continents, the bridging of an ocean. Pania felt breathless and flushed.

"We'd better get back," whispered Pania.

Jabu held her hand as if she was his. As if he would never let her go. She caught a glimpse of the evening star above them. Was it Venus? She wondered how often he had looked at that bright planet, from some exotic African setting. She sighed. Perhaps she could visit him there someday. But first, they had to get out of this forest that seemed to have swallowed them whole.

"I read somewhere that you can work out your bearings by closely observing the reflection of the moonlight off leaves," said Pania, wondering if that might come in handy.

"How exactly does it work?"

"I have no idea!"

They both burst into silly laughter.

Pania liked how cradled her hand felt in Jabu's, as they approached the huddled figures crouched around the fire. Their hands fitted neatly together. Jabu's fingers applied gentle pressure. Warm. Reassuring.

Kyle looked up from stoking the fire. His green eyes narrowed into slits. Pania felt his gaze take in their hand-holding and flame-lit smiles. He stared at the two of them, his expression difficult to read in the flickering light. Pania averted her eyes, then glanced back again. His gaze burned with condemnation. Jabu slipped his arm around her waist. He was beaming as if he had won a prize, which marginally irked her.

"What d'you get?" asked Kyle, still glaring at them.

"Just these," said Jabu, passing him a handful of leaves. Kyle put them into the pot of recently boiled water.

The four of them sat around the fire, waiting for the tea to brew. An uncomfortable silence stretched out, like ice on a windscreen. A *ruru* hooted in the distance as if life on the mountain had not been turned upside down.

"So," said Kyle, breaking the silence, "You guys a couple now?"

Jabu turned to Pania and beamed. "Are we?" he asked her.

"Before I answer that, what's with you, Kyle?" she asked. "You've been salty this whole trip."

"Surely you can figure that out," he said, poking the fire with a stick.

She blushed. All this time, Pania had thought Kyle was a friend. Someone she had a special connection with. They both cared about kids and tried to make a difference in the world through sport; through their passions. They were kindred spirits in a way, but she had never thought of him as anything more than a bud. A mentor even. To think that he felt something for her made her feel ashamed. Had she unintentionally given him false signals? Hurting him had never occurred to her.

Pania thought back to how they had met in the surf at Piha. He was chatty. He had mentioned he was surfing in a tournament the next day. She had come down to Piha to watch him, and he had won it. They had grabbed a celebratory burger together at the local cafe and talked for hours. It was comfortable with Kyle. He had told her all about Kids Surf 4 Life, and she shared about Aotearoa Ora Adventures. At their core, they were so similar. But she had never felt an attraction to him. How had she not noticed that his attention was more than mere common interest?

"I, I thought we were good friends, Kyle? You're … quite a bit older than me and I…" Pania shrugged and raised her palms. She was out of words.

"Dude," said Jabu, "I'm sorry. I never realised… I wouldn't have…"

Kyle shook his head. "After all we've been through, brother. I thought after all we've been through that you'd — I dunno, read me better. I didn't think I needed to spell things out to you. But hey, you two obviously have something going. I just feel stupid. I'm going to shutup now."

"Come on guys," said Nikau, playing the clown, "She's not even a babe. My sis. How about you forget about romance and let's all be sweet. We're not going to get out of here alive if we aren't a tight unit."

"Don't speak about your sister like that," growled Jabu.

"Do you mind gentlemen! I've had enough of being talked about as if I'm not even here. I'm going for a walk. See if I can find some forest kai. And when I come back, you'd better have calmed your farms. Far out!"

Pania charged off into the bushes, ignoring their shouts for her.

"Come back, Pania!" shouted Nikau. "The forest is not safe! Come back!" his voice pleaded.

She could hear Jabu and Kyle calling after her too. Then someone came running towards her. And panting. It was Jabu. "Come back, we're sorry," he said, resting his hand tentatively on her arm. Pania felt overwhelmed — by her feelings for him, by her shame at not realising Kyle's feelings for her. She felt angry at the way they had spoken about her as if she was an object. Her brother's words stung too.

"I need a moment alone, to make sense of my thoughts," she said quietly, shrugging off his arm and walking away.

He looked like a puppy, watching his owner leaving for work.

"But it's getting dark," said Jabu.

"Still dusk," she said, "and moonlight," looking up at the perigee moon, illuminating the forest in a silvery light.

"But still. It'll be night soon. And if a cloud blows over…"

"I've got the lighter," she said.

"How long will you be?"

"I'll be right back. I'll forage for something for us to eat. Keep an eye on Nikau, please."

"How will you find your way back?" asked Jabu.

"Keep the fire burning — I'll keep it in sight," she said, turning to go.

Jabu plodded back to the group, his shoulders stooped. Pania pressed on, into the half light of a forest, where trees were either sentinels or giants, and ferns were feathery creatures. In dim light, all forms are mutable, shape-shifting figments of ones primeval fears. Still, Pania stormed off at pace.

24

THE CAVE

PANIA

They hadn't eaten a morsel since Rusty's possum stew the previous night. Pania tried to focus on foraging and blocked out her tumultuous thoughts. Her mind kept returning to Jabu. The kiss. And to Kyle's revelation. Coming between their friendship was never her intention. She would need to calm her thoughts before returning to the group. Somehow, she would have to unify them. Divisiveness could split up the group, hampering their chance of survival.

Pania's stomach ached with hunger. If she could return with edible plants; that may be the balm they all needed. She needed to find some *miro* berries. *Nana told me they're red.* She tried to remember Nana's voice. "You can eat them in early winter," she had said. But how would she see their colour in the silky dusk? She would feel for them, smooth balls feel different from leaves and bark. *What about ureure? I don't suppose I'll find any of those, they're a spring fruit...*

She continued to roam beneath a canopy of tōtara and *rimu* trees, scavenging for kai. Volcanic ash sifted down like flour through a sieve, veiling the forest in mat grey. Dense foliage and humus reflected a muted lunar sheen, lending an apocalyptic eeriness to the surrounds.

Avoiding gorse and prickly *mingimingi*, she fingered the leaves and branches of shrubs and vines. A swooshing sound above startled her. She looked up to see an emerald kererū gliding above in a berry-full belly flash of white. *If only I had a bow and arrow*, she mused. But she would have to be starving to eat a protected bird. She turned back to comb through the scrub, hoping to find something edible. Even the young shoot of a *toetoe* would stave off her craving for sweetness.

Her feet padded through the creeping moss, parting spleenwort and maidenhair ferns. She sifted with the hands of an ancient gatherer, leaning in to scrutinise the leaves. Then, kneeling to examine a plant, Pania saw something out of place. A footprint in the moss. Large, deep and muddy. She spun around.

"Anyone there?" she called out.

Darkness enveloped her. Night had fallen now. In the distance, Pania heard a ruru calling. She waited. A mate replied from a low branch above her. She glanced up at the glow of a petite owl's eyes in the pearly light. Her focus returned to the footprint. In the moonlight, she could vaguely make out another imprint a long stride ahead, and then a few more. She followed them, wondering to herself if they might belong to Rusty, the recluse. But then she remembered his flax woven sandals, wrapped around his bare feet. She examined the deep tread of the print, moulded by walking boots. Long feet, possibly those of a tall man. A thin veneer of ash covered the fresh indentations. She was not alone in the forest. Pania shuddered.

Her pulse quickened. She surveyed her immediate surroundings. Were the shadowy figures around her the shapes of trees and ferns, or something more sinister?

Settle down, girl, she told herself. They could be a tramper's footprints.

Pania looked back. She could see the faint distant glow of the fire she had carelessly left behind, not long before. She planned to turn back to the others soon, but curiosity led her to follow the tracks a while longer. They might even lead her to a tramping path. She may even find people with food.

The moss patch ended, and the footprints disappeared. Pania rested her hand against the generous trunk of a tōtara but recoiled as her palm landed on a soft furry tail. Thinking it a possum, she lurched backwards. She tripped over a gnarled log and twisted her ankle.

"Damn-it!"

Crumpled on the moist undergrowth, Pania flicked the lighter and focused her eyes on the tree trunk. She had touched one of Rusty's possum tails, nailed to the bark. She remembered him explaining that he posted them as signposts for something useful. The route to a cave — suitable for overnight shelter, or a track to the river where he fished and found his way to town. Encouraged, she dusted off the leaves and ash and limped forward, scratching her arms on gorse as she pressed on. The rain was coming. She could smell it.

At that moment, a gust of wind ruffled the leaves above. A cloud swallowed the moonlight. Pania gasped. She had taken for granted how the light of a perigee moon had illuminated the forest. Now the deep darkness swamped her. Looking back for the fire, Pania realised she had gone too far. She squinted into the night but could see nothing. No distant amber flicker. Not even smoke. Only the dense shadows of trees, blacker than the darkness around them, and the moist smell of the forest.

Pania began to limp in what she hoped was the way back to the group. She took a few laboured steps. The pain was sharp whenever she put pressure on her ankle. She would have to crawl through the blackness as if blind and lame. She squirmed through the undergrowth of wild strawberries and creeping moss, on hands and knees.

A scuttling noise stopped Pania in her tracks. *A spider?* It would have to be enormous! *A wētā? Not a good time to have an insect phobia,* she told herself. At best it was a shy nocturnal Kiwi. She placed one hand down and then the other, edging forward, dreading what her palms might land on. Rain began to patter down. It started as a gentle drizzle and soon fell wetly. Within minutes Pania was dripping like laundry left out in a storm. Her hands and knees sloshed through mud and mucky, drenched leaves.

I'm such a fool. Why did I have to leave in a huff? She scolded herself.

A determined wind rustled treetop leaves and dragged a cloud away from the moon. Pania tried to get her bearings. Ahead of her, the ground began to incline. She had reached the base of a cliff. There, only metres in front of her, the entrance to a cave offered shelter from the rain.

Pania stood up and hobbled towards the entrance. Enormous mossy boulders formed a tunnel that narrowed into a black hole. An overhanging rock protruded over the cave, lending it a grand appearance. It reminded Pania of the abode of a wizard.

At least she could go back to the others with news of shelter. She crawled into the cave to investigate, wincing as her ankle bashed against a rock.

No sooner than she had propped herself against a cave wall, Pania got the feeling that she was not alone. The ceiling of the cave was a universe of stars, flickering their bluish-green lights. Glow-worms were harmless but got her thinking about what other creatures might be in the cave. A million possibilities flashed through her mind.

The last remaining undiscovered Moa? Bats? Bigfoot? She laughed aloud. Then she heard a muffled sound coming from the opposite wall of the cave. It was the sound of something breathing. It breathed in, and out. Pania slid her hand into her pocket and pulled out the lighter. She flicked it once. It sparked. Had the gas run out? The asthmatic breathing continued. Was this the man who had left the footsteps? The crazed hunter? Was he asleep?

Pania's heart began to race as if it would burst from her chest. She sat still, trying to inhale without a sound.

Flick. Flick. Flick.

Nothing. Only swampy darkness and the sound of chesty breathing.

25

TURNCOAT

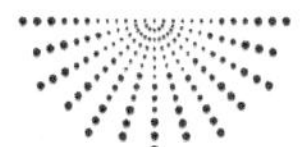

PANIA

In the dank, swampy darkness, Pania's thumb rolled over the lighter. Flick. Flick. Flick. This time the lighter ignited and Pania saw the gaunt face of a man, staring in her direction. She jumped to her feet and tried to limp for the exit but her ankle buckled under the exertion and she tumbled to the stone floor.

"I'll catch you if you try to run with that limp," he said. "It's not worth it. Be sensible. Sit down and have some manners."

Pania recognised the voice, but couldn't remember where she had heard it before. So familiar.

"A convenient turn of events, you stumbling into my cave," he said with a gruff snort. "Chuck us that lighter." It was an order.

She did as she was told. The voice had authority over her. It filled her with a deep primitive fear that made her feel like a child who dared not be disobedient.

He held the lighter to his colourless face and lit a cigarette. His eyes narrowed as he inhaled. They were ghostly green. Like Axel's eyes. He passed her the smoke.

"No, thanks," she said.

"You always were a goody-two-shoes."

Now she knew it for sure. It was Axel. He used to say that to her, when she refused to go along with one of his reckless ideas. "Have a swig of my beer," he would say. Or, "Here, take the wheel while I light my smoke."

"No way!" she would answer. And he would shake his head with disappointment and say, "You're a goody-two-shoes like your Ma."

"Axel..." she said, almost to herself.

"Why can't you call me Dad!" he yelled, losing his temper.

She wanted to tell him that he had lost the right to be called Dad when he hurt her and Ma. That Dads are kind, and he wasn't. That Dads were supposed to keep their little princesses safe from every danger, not be the danger. He was a monster, and she hated him.

Pania decided it was safest to play the game she played as a girl. Go along with him. Placate him until the temper passed, and then she could sullenly go back to gaining something of herself.

"Okay, have it your way," she said, lowering her pitch to hide the fear. "What on earth are you doing here, Dad?"

"Well, young lady, that's a long story. But you're not going anywhere."

The dim flame from the lighter revealed the remnants of a fire. A neat edging of stones circled charred logs and ash. Pania wondered if Axel had been in the cave the previous night.

"What's this? Someone's been here," he said, perplexed. "Must've been that crazy recluse. He'd better not come back. This is my cave now!" Axel scanned the cave with the lighter and found a collection of wood and kindling. "He thinks he bloody owns this forest. Well now he has a neighbour, and he'll have to suck it up." Axel was talking to himself. Then he turned to Pania. "Don't sit there like Lord Muck. Give us a hand with the fire."

Pania crawled over to the woodpile, feeling her way across the damp, slimy stones beneath her. She fumbled for a broken branch and chucked it over to the pile of sticks that Axel was building where the previous fire had been.

"Ouch! Damn wētā!" yelled Axel, looking at a bleeding finger. The impressive insect had sunk a mandible into his finger. He tried to smash the wētā with a log, but it scuttled under the pile of wood.

It has more right to be here than you, thought Pania, but managed to control her tongue.

Axel seemed freaked out by the wētā and lit the kindling. It ignited into flame. He added a couple of logs. Soon there was a blaze that lit up the damp enclosure. A long-legged spider scuttled away from the flame to a dark recess. *Remind me not to sit in that corner*, thought Pania.

With the light from the flames illuminating the space, she assessed her situation. She was in a shallow cave with her deranged father. Water dripped down a rock face in a chamber that smelled dank and smoky. There were fireflies on the ceiling, wētās on the walls and spiders in the woodpile. Her skin crawled at her surroundings, but she tried to breathe deeply and remain calm.

Axel sucked his bleeding finger, looking agitated. He scratched and picked at the skin on his nose. She noticed encrusted sores on his blemished face, perhaps from picking. It seemed his skin was crawling too as if the insects had triggered an uncontrollable impulse.

His facial expressions distorted in the flickering light. He reminded Pania of the photos of P-addicts her health teacher had shown her. Clothes hung off his wire coat hanger frame, and he was shivering, despite the fire. She suspected he had become addicted to meth. It fit with everything she had learnt. Violence, agitation, crawling skin, weight loss.

Pania doubted he would be reasonable. It was unlikely she would be able to talk her way out of the cave, and if she tried to run, he could pounce on her in an instant.

He slid a sharp knife from a holster on his belt and began to calve a spearhead out of a long branch from the woodpile. He looked menacing.

"So, Pania, did Nikau tell you how he stole from me?"

She focused on the fire, trying not to react.

"Well he did," Axel continued, "He's a chip off the old block. I told him to deliver me my stash, but what did he do? He went and hid it somewhere. Gave me an empty tin. He's a rat."

"What, when?" asked Pania.

"Ah, after I came out of the slammer."

"He didn't tell me that you were out of prison," said Pania, trying to keep her voice even.

"I bet he didn't. Probably a lot he hasn't told you eh? Did he tell you that I followed him down here? I don't suppose he mentioned that I was on the mountain."

Pania's heart felt heavy. Her efforts to reform Nikau had been in vain. She had thought she was winning the battle with him. Helping him to make the right choices.

"I, I don't believe you..." said Pania, hoping Axel was lying.

"Yep. Nikau dug it out of the yard," he continued. "My business setup fund. But the little stinker thinks he can run off and start his own business. He's got a thing coming."

"Maybe he hid it because... because he wants you to stop... doing what you do..."

"Ah yeah, that's what he says, but it's bull!"

"Okay, calm down, Ax... I mean, Dad."

"I am calm," he said, shaving a sharp point on his new spear. His eyes were sunken deep in dark pits. A vein stood out on his forehead. "I have a plan."

"Dare I ask?" said Pania.

"You're bait!" he said, and then he began to laugh hoarsely. "He'll come looking for you, won't he. You two were always close. Too close. Like an alliance. He'll come."

"And then what?"

There was a long silence. The burning logs popped and crackled, and in the distance, a ruru hooted. The smoke in the cave made Pania's eyes water, and she began to cough.

"I'm figuring it out," he grunted. "Now a man needs his shut-eye. Move around to this side of the fire. Sit on my left so you can't make a run for the exit."

Pania hesitated.

"Move it!" he shouted.

Reluctantly, she shuffled over and sat down beside him, feeling cold inside, despite the fire. So cold and hard. She was trapped beside the man who had made her life a misery so often. The school counsellor had helped her to get over the trauma of her childhood. But here she was, a hostage. She closed her eyes and prayed.

"Father God, please Lord, help me…"

It seemed like moments later that Pania awoke to voices calling her name. She had drifted into an exhausted slumber, and many hours had passed. She berated herself for falling asleep. She had wanted to wait for the moment that Axel fell asleep so that she could slip out of the cave. She looked over at him. He was snoring now, his head slumped on his chest. And voices were calling her name, nearby. This was her moment. She began to move, but his left hand had a hold on her arm. As she shifted, he stirred, and his grip tightened. She sat still, hoping he would nod off again.

"Pania! Pania, where are you?" came a voice, not far from the cave.

Axel was now awake and foul-tempered. He grabbed her arm tightly and said, "This is when you call out, 'I'm in here, help me.'" His voice turned into a fake high pitch at the end. Then it turned gruff. "Use your best maiden in distress cry."

"And what if I don't?" asked Pania. She wrestled with wanting to be rescued, and not wanting to lure Nikau and her friends into this sticky web.

He laughed, showing his rotten teeth. "Then you're stuck with me."

In the dim light of the embers, his pale eyes looked yellow. The ice in her veins froze almost solid. She despised him.

"Nikau! Jabu! Help! I'm in here! Help me!" she screamed. It was no act. The louder she screamed, the more desperately Pania wanted the boys to find her. She heard footsteps stomping up the path to the entrance. They were calling her name. Her brother. Jabu. Kyle. They appeared in the archway.

A gust of wind cleared the sky for an instant. The moonlight that fell on the young men was like a beam of daylight. How handsome and heroic they all looked. Jabu, her Zulu heartthrob, stood on the left of the cave entrance. His braids neatly tied back into a ponytail, his round, honest eyes scanning the scene. He was flanked by Nikau, her baby brother, whose pale green eyes slid from Pania to Axel, lazily. He was a handsome young Māori man, and she loved him so. But who was he really? Where did his loyalty lie? Kyle, a typical blonde, tanned surfer, was the tallest of the three. She remembered that Kyle had admitted to having feelings for her. She lowered her gaze.

At that moment, she felt like she was Pirongia, the Māori Princess and these were the mountain warriors, here to battle for her.

"About time, fellas," said Axel, flashing his shining dagger for them to see. Then he pressed it into Pania's side. She gasped. All the joy at seeing the boys evaporated.

"He is poking a knife in my side. Please, come in, sit down and co-operate," she said in a low murmur.

"Easy," said Jabu, doing as he was told. Kyle looked poised for a fight. Pania remembered that he had spent time in the South African army, and she hoped he would not try to be a hero. He glared at Axel and crouched beside Jabu at the far wall of the cave as if ready to pounce. Nikau stood in the doorway, looking casual and noncommittal.

"Hi Dad," he said, cheerfully.

"Sit!" said Axel.

Nikau slid down the wall next to Kyle.

"Wassup?" he asked.

"Well, well, well," said Axel. "This is quite a family reunion." His eyes went from Nikau to Pania and back. "I didn't expect to feel this emotional." His voice cracked, surprisingly. He wiped a real tear from his cheek. "First time I've had both my kids with me in years. I could do without the doe-eyed suitors though. You two, scram," he said, addressing Jabu and Kyle.

Pania was not moved by Axel's momentary display of sentiment. He had always been labile. One minute he would be a bully, and the next, he was all tears and apologies. It meant nothing to her. There was no substance to his mood swings.

"Who are you?" asked Jabu, "And why would I leave Pania here with you?"

"He's our... Dad," said Pania in a low voice.

"And I'm gonna teach these kids some respect," he said, looking manic.

"Respect is earned, not demanded," said Pania, forgetting her passive pretence.

"Is that right, princess?" jeered Axel, squeezing her arm so tightly that it bruised.

Pania wiped away a flood of tears "Stay back," she said to Jabu and Kyle, who looked like they were ready for a battle.

"Go on, get," said Axel. "She doesn't love you. Either of you pretenders. Now, I'm the Dad, and I'm more than a little protective. I hope I don't have to ask you again."

Pania flicked her head back and moved her eyes in the direction of the cave exit like she meant it.

"C'mon, Jabu," said Kyle. He got up to leave, and Jabu followed reluctantly.

"You'd better not hurt them," said Jabu. "We'll be calling the cops as soon as we get out of this forest. Be sensible man."

Jabu turned as he left, making eye contact with Pania. She knew he wouldn't go far. She expected they would hide out somewhere near the cave and figure out their next move.

Minutes passed in silence. The echoing cave felt hollow without Jabu, like an empty casket. Axel began to rekindle the fire.

"So, here's my plan. I'm taking your sister back to Auckland, and she is going to let me into the house when nobody's there. I will turn it upside down to find what is mine. If it's not there, she's gonna cop your flak," he said.

A wētā scuttled out of a pile of sticks. Axel flicked it into the fire where it sizzled.

"No, no, the stash is not in the house, Dad," said Nikau in a friendly voice. "Why would you want to endure a trip to Auckland with this nag bag when I can tell you where it is?"

"I can see what you're trying to do, son," said Axel.

"No, seriously. And I've been thinking about what you said about the family business. Nikau sauntered around the fire, over to them. He knelt down and whispered loudly to Axel. In the stillness of the night, Pania could hear his poisonous words.

"I've hidden the stash in a hut in the forest. I can lead you there."

"That madman's hut!" yelled Axel. "What the hell? How're we supposed to get it off him? He has a rifle." Nikau rolled his eyes towards Pania as if to say, "Remember, she is listening." He whispered again. Pania only overheard a few words this time. Something about leading him there and waiting for Rusty to go possum hunting.

"Why the turn around?" said Axel.

Nikau leaned close and whispered in his ear again. Pania overheard "fresh start", "family business" and "Australia".

She felt sick. Nikau was choosing Axel over her and Papa Joe and Ma and embracing a life of filthy crime and betrayal. Electing to team up with his delusional father and sell drugs and run from the police. A tear of bitter disappointment welled up and ran down her cheek. She had an acidic taste in her mouth and wanted to gag.

Axel began to laugh. First, it was a low chuckle. Nikau giggled. Then it became a hearty guffaw. His whole body shook with laughter, and Nikau, reclining at his side, joined in.

"Oh, you're something else," said Axel when his shuddering laughter had stopped. "First you steal my stash and pretend you're trying to get me to come clean, and now you've realised you actually need a partner, right?"

"Right," said Nikau, smiling awkwardly.

"You thought you could outwit your old man. You sly fox. I like it."

"Partners?" asked Nikau.

"Partners," said Axel, and patted Nikau hard on the back.

"Now get out of here, Pania," said Nikau coldly. "Go and catch up with your boyfriends. And when you get out, tell the cops we're dead. We died in the volcano."

"For once, do what you're told," said Axel, giving her a shove. Pania fell forward and almost landed in the hot embers. She climbed to her feet slowly, taking her time, dusting off the ash and glaring at them. *The snakes.* Then she hobbled to the threshold, trying to hide her limp.

At the cave entrance, she turned and fixed Nikau with her fiercest glare. "I should say, 'you're dead to me'. But I can't. Get a grip bro."

FAMILY SECRETS

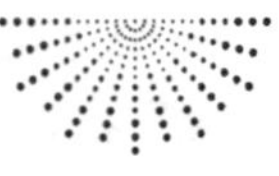

NIKAU

A dense cloud obscured the moon. Once again, a sooty blackness suffocated the writhing woods. The shadowy forest had become, in the night, an entity. The darkness, and the sulphurous forest, had a dripping, acrid presence — alive with creeping dendrites and beasts scurrying through the undergrowth. Wet snow began to fall.

Axel's sinewy fingers bruised Nikau's arm as they shuffled and stumbled like two blind men. Nikau was a hostage.

He remembered Pania's fierce glare. Like an overthrown queen. Haughty and devastated by the betrayal. How he wanted to get out of this forest alive, so he could tell her the truth for once. That he had lied, to save her.

"Which way?" grumbled Axel.

"I... I'm trying to retrace our path back to Rusty's shed," said Nikau. In truth, he had no idea where he was, and wondered how Axel expected him to lead them with zero visibility.

"I'm feeling the trees," said Nikau. "Rusty-the-recluse nailed possum tails on the trees, as signposts."

Give him some information, thought Nikau. *Keep his trust.*

Earlier, back in the cave, Axel had insisted they allow Pania and her 'boyfriends' half an hour head start.

"Let them find each other and clear off. I don't want them ambushing us, is all," Axel had said.

"Can't we sleep and get moving in the morning?" Nikau had asked. He had not slept. He had spent three hours after midnight, with Jabu and Kyle, searching for Pania. Moving in ever-widening concentric circles and backtracking to the fire, so that they wouldn't get lost. His energy was almost depleted.

Now they were staggering through the forest in the wee, dark hours of the morning. It began to rain. Nikau felt isolated and vulnerable without his sister and friends. He hated to admit it to himself, but he was afraid of Axel.

"C'mon boy, feel those trees… I need the stash…"

Nikau did not reply. His thoughts wandered. *All those years you were in prison, I missed you — and wished we could be together — to chat...*

"I got into hard drugs while doing a brick," said Axel, as if trying to explain his addiction.

"Doing a brick?"

"Ten years inside."

A long time, thought Nikau.

"Now I'm feeling scratchy, understand? I need a fix…"

So much we missed out on, so much I wanted to tell you; to ask you.

"When we get to the madman-you-call-Rusty, I'll give you this spear. If things turn ugly, use it."

I wanted to play rugby with you at the local park. You and me together. Not like this.

"We'll sneak up, and if he's sleeping, I'll grab his gun. If he intercepts me, spear this into his back…"

Nikau played out various scenarios. If he led Axel to Rusty's hut, the wizened old recluse could possibly help him. But it could go pear-shaped. Things could get ugly. People might cark it. Both men were mad as a meat axe. He envisaged a dagger plunged into flesh, a spear piercing organs… a shot fired, a bullet wound. No. Rusty was not the solution.

Still, they staggered as if blindfolded, arms out, feeling for trees. For possum tail signposts.

All those years I wanted to see you, to have quality time with you, thought Nikau. So many unanswered questions.

"Tell me, Axel… I mean Dad," he ventured, "since it's only you and me in this forest, can we talk, man to man?"

Axel snorted dismissively through his nose. "Sure, if you think you're a man… whatever."

Nikau breathed deeply. He had to know the truth.

"Okay, here goes… Was Ma cheating on you? Was she getting it on with Papa Joe?"

"Bloody hell, you're cocky!"

They walked in silence. Nikau could hear his father breathing through his nostrils. After a pause, Axel spoke.

"If you must know, no, she wasn't," he said. Do you think I'm the kind of man whose wife cheats on him? She wouldn't have dared!"

Nikau reeled. He had spent his whole young life, believing that Papa Joe was the reason his Dad had left them.

"So, why did you leave us?" he whispered.

"So many questions…"

"Look, it's just you and me in these dark woods. Who knows if we'll even make it out," said Nikau.

Axel sighed. "I have a temper son. It's my only weakness. Your Ma knew how to wind me up. Always nagging and fussing about something. She's neurotic. I guess I slapped her around a bit. I was always sorry after," he said shrugging. "But one day she called Joe through the window. He was there in a flash. None of his business. Talk about a nosey neighbour. We had a bit of a 'how's your father?'"

"And so you gapped it?"

"Afraid so."

Eleven years of silence.

"But why didn't you ever visit us?" *All those years, no phone calls, no letters, not a single visit. Surely you came out on parole?*

"Sheez — the lies in this family get my goat! Didn't your Ma tell you there was a trespassing order against me? They went to the cops. I'm not supposed to come near you. Or your Ma, or Pania for that matter."

"Why?" asked Nikau. *Did you hurt Pania?* These words didn't reach his lips but tattooed themselves on his heart.

"Too bloody PC, that's why. A Father can't even discipline his own."

Nikau remembered the look of fear on Pania's face when she had sat beside Axel in the cave. As if he was the last person on earth that she wanted to be holed up with. He had never seen his determined sister looking so defenceless.

Personally, he had no nasty memories of his Dad. He remembered being hoisted upon a branch in a tree he had wanted to climb. A few blurry ideas, but nothing negative. Perhaps he was too young to remember.

"Why didn't they tell me?" he asked.

All the lies, Nikau thought. *So many family secrets.*

"They're up themselves is why. Probably wanted to raise you without knowing some of the ugly truths about your old man. But let me tell you something..." Axel put his unshaven face up against

Nikau's ear. He could feel the bristles and smell the man's sour breath. "You were my favourite, boy. I never laid a hand on you."

Nikau felt ill. All the lies Ma and Pania and Papa Joe had told, to protect him from the wretched truth. His biological father was a violent man, a man without a conscience.

"Now I need your help, son. To be honest, I'm an addict, okay. And if I don't get hold of that stash soon, I'm going to start having serious withdrawal."

Nikau completed the puzzle he was piecing together. When Axel couldn't be head of a family, he went off the rails and got into drugs. Now it seemed he was a slave to his addiction. Narcotics were his cruel master.

Nikau noticed Axel shivering. He remembered learning about meth addicts and hypothermia at school. For a change, he must have been paying attention to that lesson.

Like Gollum yearning for the ring, only one prize would appease his Dad. If they found the hut and Axel discovered the stash was not there, it would not be pretty.

Think. Plan something. What are my options? Nikau asked himself. *Must I take him on? Punch him square in the jaw. A right uppercut. Grab the dagger.* He pictured someone bleeding, face down in the mud. *No. No, not that.*

Axel cursed violently. He had banged his head on a tree. "This is bull! I'm getting seriously pissed." He grabbed Nikau by the shoulders and shook him fiercely. "Where the hell are you leading me?"

That temper he told me about. Poor Pania. Poor Ma. All those years...

Nikau pictured his ancestors from *Tūwharetoa Iwi*, hunting Moa in this forest. Bare-chested, muscular and fearless. They would have been nimble too. Leaping and bounding over rocks and climbing ravines. He wondered if he could dig deep and will their ancient strength into his muscles and sinews. The power of believing that he came from strong tribesmen. Men with *mana*.

He decided that it wasn't cowardly to run, but wise. He was young and swift-footed, and this was his natural advantage. He needed a head start. To create some distance between them.

He heard a gurgling noise up ahead. The sound of the arterial river that Rusty had told them about. This would lead to the Mangaturu-turu River, which would, in turn, guide them out of the forest. His heart leapt. The dense night was fading into the ashy grey of morning, and a *tui* sang out an electronic greeting to the new day. It chimed up at the endnote in a different dialect to the tui's song back home.

Home. He could see it in his mind's eye. Papa Joe in hospital, dear man. *Ma must be worried sick about us.* Surely the eruptions had been in the newspapers. There might be a search party. But he couldn't wait for rescuers to find them. They were both freezing and weak. Hunger and thirst nagged at him.

Could he persuade Axel that he had been lying and that he had thrown the stash away? He looked across at the face of the frightful man, avoiding his wildly staring eyes. Axel ground his jaw and dug his fingers in Nikau's arm, twitching sporadically. His Dad was not a reasonable man, nor was he in a sane state of mind. That much was obvious. Telling him the truth was not an option.

The roiling river was only a few strides ahead. Nikau could see a natural weir of mossy rocks, inviting a careful crossing.

Now he knew what he had to do.

THE RIVER

NIKAU

A steep and slippery drop-off fell to the river below.

"We need to cross here," Nikau said.

Axel released Nikau from his grip, grabbing hold of a protruding root to prevent him from sliding into the river. Nikau knew this was his chance. He needed to gain enough ground to be out of arm's reach. He slid down the bank ahead of Axel. If he nimbly crossed the rocky weir and reached the other side with space, he could clamber up the far bank and make a run for it.

"Stay close to me boy," grumbled Axel, as Nikau hopped from rock to rock. Nikau almost lost his footing on the second to last rock. His foot slipped sideways on the moss, but he made a quick adjustment and bounded to the next one. This rock wobbled under his foot, and he fell forward, managing to land with two hands stretched out, breaking his fall on the river bank.

"Hey, slow down!" shouted Axel as Nikau scurried up the bank, digging his fingers into the clay, clutching roots and shrubs. He heard a cry and a wooden thud, but he did not turn back. At the top of the bank, Nikau was about to gap it, when curiosity made him glance over his shoulder.

There in the corner of his vision, sprawled Axel. Nikau swung around. The body of his captor lay, draped across the boulders like a crash test dummy. A slippery stone made an unlikely cushion for his head. Blood streamed into the brackish water.

Nikau stood still, taking it all in. His adrenalin was surging from trying to make an escape. Now his instincts went from fight or flight into rescue mode. His surf lifeguard training kicked in. He slid down the bank, digging his heels in the clay to brake at the bottom. Was Axel dead? *My Dad.*

Yet he found his heart unmoved.

Nikau stepped into the icy, shallow water, and found a firm foothold. Then, with every last store of energy, he dragged Axel from the rocks, clasping him under the arms like he would a drowning man. He deposited the limp body at the base of the riverbank on a flat ledge below the steep rise.

Nikau listened for breathing. The breath was rasping, but even. Heartbeat? Slow. The gash in Axel's head was not deep, but sticky with blood. Nikau took off his neck warmer and wrapped it around the head wound.

"Wake up," said Nikau, nudging Axel's shoulder.

The man did not stir. Nikau examined the steep incline. There was no way he would be able to pull the weight of a man up that bank. Nada. He could not leave Axel here and look for help as the river might rise and drown the unconscious man. There had to be a way to get him onto higher ground.

What would his ancestors do? He looked around the forest for clues. Flax cords! He remembered one year they had made six-plaited cords from flax leaves as part of an inquiry lesson at school. They were learning about *Te Ao Māori*. He had mucked around until Ben started whipping his legs with a well-crafted cord. It had caused a welt. Well, then, of course, he had wanted revenge. He went to the teacher to ask her to teach him the method, though she had already been through it with the class.

"How's it done, Miss?" he had asked. He paid attention this time and copied her until he had made a strong cord. When Miss turned her attention to a group of diligent girls, Nikau had sneaked up behind Ben and returned the injury with interest. Ben clearly had a lower pain threshold than Nikau because he had screamed.

"Ayeeeeee!"

Both boys had ended up with detention. But now wasn't the time to be distracted by memories. He hauled himself up the river bank and used his penknife to cut long leaves of flax until he had a handsome pile. A quick climb back down to check if Axel was still breathing broke his progress but had to be done. Then he began the plaiting process. It was slow going, but Nikau worked steadily, focusing all his attention on his fingers at work, and the growing rope. He shivered as he worked. The water in his boots was turning to ice. Axel must be freezing too. He had to work quicker. His eyes scanned the surrounds like a *Haast* eagle. Twine! A long sinewy vine roped itself around a tree. He cut it at full stretch — up high and at the base of the tree. That gave him an extra couple of metres of rope. A good sailors knot attached the flax chord to the twine.

Nikau slid down the bank again and checked Axel's breathing. The man was shivering. His lips had turned blue. Nikau threaded the rope under Axel's back, coming up under his armpits and over his shoulders. Up the bank, he scampered, like a busy beaver at work. He dragged the rope around the base of a thin tree near the river bank. The idea was to use the tree as a pulley, abseil down the bank and use his weight and gravity to lift Axel up to the higher ground. Nikau dug his heels in and tugged. The man's mass did not budge. He heaved and perspired, leaning and digging trenches in the mud with his feet as he pushed himself backwards. It was futile. He was not strong enough.

The friction of the rope of the tree and the heavier weight of his Dad made the task impossible.

"Damn it!" he shouted at the tree and the rope. He smashed his hand into the mud.

"Do you need a hand?" came a voice from across the river. It was Pania! He swung around, grinning from ear to ear. Then he remembered her final cutting words in the cave. His smile faded.

"What ya doing here?" he asked.

Pania, Jabu and Kyle stood at the river's edge, assessing the situation.

"It could have worked if you'd had a block and tackle," said Kyle.

"Yebo. It's a good effort," said Jabu.

Nikau ignored them and considered his sister. "Pania, what are you doing here?" he asked again.

She didn't answer and began to lower herself down the far bank to the river. Jabu took Pania's hand and helped her down, with Kyle following.

"Cross carefully," said Nikau, clambering down to the river from the opposite side. "It's slippery as."

"Did he fall on the rocks," asked Pania, "or did you knock him out?"

"What do ya think of me, sis? He fell. That last rock wobbles..."

Pania stumbled, Jabu teetered, and Kyle leapt over the last rock until they clustered around Axel. Pania, like Nikau, was a qualified surf lifeguard. She listened for breathing and felt for a pulse.

Nikau had reached them, and stood over Pania, feeling awkward. "Pania?"

Pania looked up at him. "I may have been disappointed in you, but I wasn't about to leave you in the forest with this maniac," she said, tilting her head towards Axel.

"What happened in the cave," said Nikau, "well, I was lying, okay. I'm not in partnership with him. I wanted to lure him away, so you could be safe."

Pania stood up and put her arms on his shoulders. Her rich almond eyes looked into his.

"I know," she said. "I realised after we had tracked you for a while. I could see Axel was manhandling you."

"Why did you follow me then, if you still thought I was a rotter when you started out?"

Jabu joined in. "Your sister said, 'He's my baby brother, and I can't leave him in the forest, no matter how much he tries to mess up his life.' It was… touching."

Nikau flung his arms around Pania. "Thank-you," he said. She wrapped him in a sisterly hug.

"I should be thanking you, bro, you put yourself on the line for me."

"As you do," he said, pulling away from her awkwardly.

They stood in silence, assessing their unconscious birth father, and the steep bank.

"If we all work together, we can pull him up," suggested Kyle.

With a brief plan and a "three-two-one-go!" they collectively dragged and pushed him up the bank.

Once deposited on higher land, Axel puked up a stomach of water and opened his eyes. He gawked at the group, startled. The man wobbled to his feet like a newborn giraffe. He looked like the living dead. Eggshell white with a shining pate, translucent eyes set in dark hollows and a snarl curling his top lip. Blood congealed on his face. He shivered with hypothermia and shook with rage.

"What on earth do you think you're doing?" he growled.

The pendulum had swung. The group had almost depleted their strength, and Axel's sheer rage seemed to transform him into someone who could take them all on. Axel reached for his dagger and pulled it out. The blade gleamed, washed clean by the river.

"Hey, steady on," said Jabu, stepping towards him.

"Aaaargh! My head. It hurts," cried Axel, slumping to his knees and dropping the dagger. Nikau waited for him to get up. Instead, Axel moaned like a felled soldier in the trenches. He collapsed to his side, groaning and whining.

Is it a trap? Nikau wondered.

He crept over to his father, half expecting a hand to reach out and grab him.

"Are you okay?" he asked tentatively.

The voice that came from the broken man was paper-thin and grating.

"I need the stash… please… help me. I'm in terrible withdrawal…"

Nikau recoiled at the sight of his father. The man was in a cold sweat and in the grip of a relentless tremor. Were Axel's symptoms caused by the bash to the head and the merciless cold, or the unwilling drug detox? Or a combination? He looked repugnant, and Nikau was filled with loathing.

You pitiful man, he thought. *I'm not like you.* But he spoke gently. "You need a hospital. Can you walk? I know the way out of here."

"I'm not leaving here until you've taken me to the stash at the hut," grumbled Axel.

"There is no stash at the hut," said Nikau. "I lied."

"I don't… believe you," spat Axel.

"It doesn't matter what you believe. You either get up and walk out of here with us, or you'll have to wait until we get help. Now, what will it be?" asked Nikau.

Axel attempted to sit up but collapsed again.

"His shivering is insane," whispered Pania.

Nikau took his ski jacket and covered his father.

Axel's eyes rolled back, and his head flopped to one side. They watched him for a minute, dumbfounded. Axel began to drool from the corner of his mouth.

"He's lost consciousness again," said Pania.

This was serious. They had to get help.

THE MAN IN THE BOY

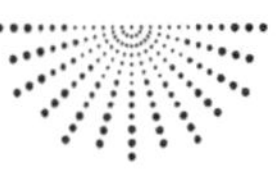

NIKAU

Nikau and Pania stood over their unconscious father. Jabu and Kyle hung a few feet back. Snow dripped off leaves and branches while the river gurgled by, oblivious of their plight.

"We can't leave him here," said Nikau. "He might die of hypothermia or something."

"Well, what do you propose we do?" asked Pania, "Carry him?"

"We could make a stretcher," suggested Nikau, looking around him for bamboo or straight branches.

"What if he wakes up while we're carrying him?" asked Jabu.

"Then we've got this, as protection," said Kyle, claiming Axel's dagger. "And we can tie his hands to the stretcher with flax."

"Are you crazy?" asked Nikau. "Imagine how pissed he would be if he woke up and found himself tied down? He might look thin, but he's strong and wiry as..."

"I say we leave him and follow the river out of here. When we find help, we can send people back to get him," said Pania, trying to take charge.

"No. We're not leaving him," said Nikau, his voice breaking.

"Father, or no father, dangerous or not... he is a man who needs our help."

"You're my baby brother, and I'm in charge of this expedition! I got you into danger, and now I'm getting you home safely, you hear?" yelled Pania. She had lost her composure and was half crying. "He's unpredictable and crazy, and he tried to kidnap us. We need to run for help, and we need to do it now!"

Nikau composed himself. His sister was usually the one with quiet authority. This time he knew he was right. If they left Axel, he might die. His sister was gripped with fear of the man, and he couldn't blame her. Axel had hurt her and their Ma, and Nikau had been none the wiser. But wicked or not, he was a man, unconscious, with hypothermia and dehydration, and he needed help. They could not waste time squabbling. He knew he was thinking more clearly than his sister, and spoke with conviction.

"Listen to me, sis. We are not leaving Axel in the forest to die."

"He won't die!"

"We don't know that. It's not the right thing to do. You know it. We are going to make a stretcher," Nikau said, gesturing to Jabu and Kyle to get started, "and we will carry this man out of the forest. We are not going to tie his hands down either. Imagine what trampers would think if they saw a bunch of kids, armed with a dagger, carrying an unconscious man, tied to a stretcher? They'd think we knocked him over the head or something."

Pania's mouth fell open as he spoke. She was silent for a moment. She looked down at Axel, who seemed utterly helpless. Her gaze returned to Nikau.

"You're right," she said, sounding surprised. Nikau watched her expression as she appraised him. It was as if she saw the man in the boy, and was wondering when the change had taken place. "Yes," she said. "You're so, so right."

"Good," said Nikau. Feeling uncomfortable with the sudden shift in the hierarchy, he asked, "Anyone know how we're going to make a stretcher, with a dagger, a penknife and a bunch of trees and stuff?"

"Muscle power," said Jabu, flexing.

"Cool. We need to work fast," said Nikau. And they did. Working as a team, they snapped and sawed and hacked at branches until they had two equal lengths. They were less than straight, but they would have to do. Flax was woven to and fro between the parallel bars. They strengthened the bed with a vine.

Nikau glanced over at Axel. He seemed paler than ten minutes ago.

"It's good enough," he said. "Let's lift him."

The four of them struggled with his dead weight.

"Put him in the recovery position," said Jabu, "then slide the stretcher behind him and roll him back on."

This worked effectively. Axel lay on the stretcher, comatose.

"Are you going to manage with your twisted ankle, Pania?" asked Jabu.

"It's feeling better," said Pania bravely. "We may need to stop for rests now and then."

"Well, if it hurts, I'll take your share of the weight," he offered.

"Right. Three, two, one… heave," said Kyle.

They each grabbed hold of one branch end, heaved the bed up, and began to march. It was heavy going, climbing over roots and ducking under low hanging vines. Sporadically Kyle had to hack through the undergrowth to make a path, often showering them all with snow. But after a time, the forest thinned out. The river sped up and surged over rapids beside them. They quickened their pace as if keeping time with the galloping waters.

The trees were laden with snow that had fluttered down during the night. Raindrops slid off leaves onto the soaked undergrowth and snow scudded off branches, slipping down the back of Nikau's neck. The river gurgled over rocks alongside him. It could have been a treasured moment, as if the forest had adorned itself in white, especially for them. For a time, Nikau forgot their circumstances. He drifted into a dreamy oneness with his surrounds, and a peace came over him.

Finally, the forest thinned out and gave way to rocks and low grasses, lichen and gaudy coloured fungi. Nikau could hear it now, the Mangaturuturu river, pounding with debris from the lahars. And there, looming nonchalantly, stood Mount Ruapehu, smoking like an elder puffing on a pipe. Black and grey plumes extended upwards, miles high. Ahead lay the river, and another rope bridge. They had only to cross bravely, and they would be on a tramping trail that would lead back to Ohakune. But Nikau remembered what had happened to the last bridge.

"Stop!" he said. The group halted and lowered the stretcher. "Let me have a look, and see if it's safe to cross," he said, holding out his hand. Nikau walked to the river's edge. He remembered the bridge higher up that was dragged away by a boulder in the lahar. The gorge was deeper here than it had been further up the mountain. Trees and rocks tumbled down the river, disturbed by the lethal flow of yesterday. It was a hazardous soup of roiling debris. But the bridge was a good twenty feet above the river.

"Okay, let's cross," said Nikau, resuming his position. They raised the stretcher and stepped gingerly onto the rope bridge. It swayed and wobbled with every step.

"Don't look down," said Pania.

Nikau hoped the wooden slats beneath them were not rotten, as they needed both hands to hold the stretcher. If the slats collapsed, they would not be able to grab the rope, holding up the bridge. They would be nothing more than flotsam and detritus. Something the mountain had coughed up. As his foot reached land at the far side of the swollen river, Nikau breathed a sigh of relief. *Not far now*, he thought.

"C'mon guys," he said, ignoring his blisters.

"Yeah, keep going," said Jabu. "We can do this."

They were following a well-maintained trampers path. Soon they reached a signpost pointing to the end of a trail. The forest continued to live and breathe behind them, the mountain loomed to their left, and as the trees around them thinned out, a vista opened up ahead. In the distance was a road.

NOT OUT OF THE WOODS YET

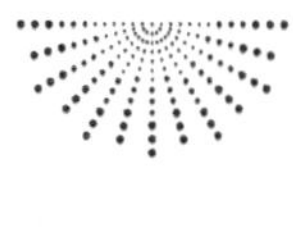

NIKAU

A DAY LATER

As the distance to home fell away, Nikau's longing grew. The desert road stretched out before them. Soon they had left the land of mountain warriors behind. He glimpsed Ruapehu and Tongariro in the rearview mirror. They passed the pleasant hill, named Pirongia. Later the van followed the perimeter of the supervolcano, Taupō. This time they stopped for takeaways in town. Nikau murdered a burger.

After lunch, Pania drove on, through Rotorua, where superheated geothermal activity simmered shallowly. Vents let off steam, geysers erupted superheated water, and the sulphurous smell reminded them of the lava chambers not far below. The landscape became pastoral and tranquil as they left the extraordinary central north island behind them. The van circumnavigated the city of Hamilton. Six hours after leaving Ohakune, they reached the city of Auckland.

Pania dropped off Areta, Tipene, then Ben. Meaningful hugs were exchanged. After that, they said goodbye to Jabu and Kyle at a motel.

Pania held Jabu for what seemed like half an hour to Nikau. Meanwhile, Kyle busied himself looking for the motel keys in his backpack. Nikau looked the other way. The romance was nauseating.

After twenty minutes on the highway, Pania took an offramp to the suburbs, then swung a left turn into their street. In a few hundred metres, they would be home. He imagined a bracing bear hug from Papa Joe, and a tearful embrace from Ma, followed by hot *kai*. Later, he would have to decide how much of the truth to tell them.

Pania had gone quiet after saying goodbye to Jabu. They sat in silence as she drove past rows of wooden houses. A man walked his dog, a teen shot hoops. They swerved around a tiny old woman, who pushed a trolley full of market goods into the street.

A police vehicle was stationed outside their house, where Pania usually parked her car. She had to pull in further down the road. The last few steps along the sidewalk, carrying backpacks felt tiresome to Nikau's weary legs. As he sidled next to the police car, he wondered if the neighbours had strife.

"We're home!" shouted Nikau, throwing the door open and stepping aside to let his sister in first. Pania stepped through the threshold and froze, startled. Nikau charged into the room behind her and stopped dead. A policeman and a man in plainclothes sat on armchairs opposite Papa Joe and Ma, who sat side by side on the sofa. The conversation halted abruptly the minute they walked in. An uncomfortable silence arrested the room. Ma's teary eyes flashed at Nikau, as if in a warning.

A middle-aged man stood up and walked over to Nikau and Pania, instructing them to sit down. He reminded Nikau of a walrus.

"I'm detective Stokes. Maybe you can tell us about this," he said, holding up a vacuum pack bag bulging with blue pills. He wore rubber gloves and held the bag as if it were toxic.

The stash!

Nikau said nothing. His eyes met Pania's, and she gave him a steady look and a barely noticeable nod. He had told her everything on the trip home.

"We told these coppas we know nothing about this stuff," said Ma, flustered. "Their sniffer dog found it in our bin outside."

"Quiet, Miss," said the young constable.

Papa Joe stared at Nikau below hooded eyes. Nikau could not decipher the expression. Was it distrust? Anger? Or was he resigned to the idea that Nikau knew the answer to the question?

Nikau felt ill. He would have to tell the story about how he had dug up the tin. All he wanted was to be right with Papa Joe. For a fresh start.

"Listen carefully, kids," said the detective. "Our narcotics unit happened to be walking their sniffer dog up this street..."

"Looking for P-Labs!" interrupted Ma.

The policemen both shot her a look of disapproval.

"And their dog took an interest in your bin. The narcs fished this out. They sent a sample away for testing, and well, this is nasty stuff. Methamphetamine with some horse tranquiliser and other chemicals in the mix. The next step is to take fingerprints." He knitted his brow and fixed them both with a steely glare. "I hope none of your fingerprints will be on the bag. You seem like a nice family."

"We're also going to need urine samples from you all," added the younger constable imperiously.

"Perhaps," said the detective, staring pointedly at Nikau, "If ONE of you knows something, they may be able to save a lot of trouble for the rest of ya."

Nikau looked over at Pania. She nodded reassuringly.

"I..., I can tell you everything," said Nikau, wringing his hands.

"Excuse me, detective," interrupted Papa Joe. "We've been worried sick about our kids for days. They were up on that volcano. We only heard yesterday that they survived. Can we come around later to place a statement? We need some family time."

"No, sorry. Too much chance for you all to collaborate on a story. We need to hear your son out now," said the detective gravely.

"Ah well let me at least give them a hug," said Joe, standing tall and stepping over to the kids as if he refused to take 'no' for an answer.

"My son," he said to Nikau, squeezing the air out of his lungs and rustling his hair. Ma jumped up and gave Nikau a soppy hug and kiss, and then they both turned their attention to Pania.

The constable examined his polished boots, uncomfortable.

"Right, now tell us your story, young man. This is an official police statement." Both interrogators took out pens and notebooks and began scribbling as Nikau spoke.

Nikau started the story at the beginning, the day Axel was released from prison and showed up on his walk to school. He continued, explaining the instructions to dig up a tin, and how conflicted he had felt. He kept looking over to Ma and Papa Joe and mouthing, "Sorry…" Pania sat on the arm of a chair, beside him, her hand on his back. Whenever he stumbled or faltered, she encouraged him — helping him to find his words. He told them how he had thrown the stash into the bin outside, hoping to keep his father out of trouble.

Nikau launched into the story about the mountain, and how Axel had followed him down there. He was thankful that Pania could join in now, sharing her side of the story. Half an hour passed. The constable kept asking the detective how to spell words, some simple, some challenging. The detective asked pointed questions, trying to trip them up, glaring at them under bushy eyebrows.

"Tea?" asked Ma.

"Coffee if you have it, Miss," said the constable.

"Tea would be lovely, thanks," answered Stokes, softening.

Ma brought a tray of tea, coffee and biscuits for the group.

Between mouthfuls, the story unfolded… about Axel's attempts to co-opt Nikau into his 'family business'.

"That low-life scoundrel," growled Papa Joe.

"Continue," said detective Stokes.

Nikau told them about the volcano, and the avalanche, and how he thought Pania had died. His voice trembled, and he began to shake. Then Nikau cried. He remembered how he had felt, standing alone near the summit of Ruapehu, facing a wall of snow, suspecting Pania had been swallowed up.

"It's okay, bro. I'm here," said Pania, rubbing his back.

Ma got up and put her arms around them both. "My *tamariki*," she said.

"Thank you, Lord," said Papa Joe, looking skyward.

The detective cleared his throat. The constable took his reading glasses off and wiped them on his shirt.

Pania filled in the story for a while, as Nikau went to the bathroom. When he returned, they told the policemen about Rusty the recluse, and Axel's cave. About how Axel had tried to kidnap them. Pania said what a hero Nikau had been, tricking Axel into letting her go.

"It was the longest night of my life," said Nikau. "I didn't know whether to lead him to Rusty, or fight him, or run. I decided to bolt, but he fell behind me as we crossed a river and hit his head on a rock. He was out cold!"

Pania explained how they had arrived on the scene and helped drag Axel up the river bank to dry land.

"We made him a stretcher. And we carried him out of the forest. Meanwhile, we didn't know that rescue workers had been looking for us ever since the first eruption," said Nikau.

"Yeah, Areta and Tipene and Ben had managed to get down the ski lifts okay. After an hour or so, they told the ski lift staff that we hadn't come down. They sent snowploughs and helicopters with spotlights to look for us. They scoured the mountain and the forest. Eventually, they sent people on foot, but they had no idea where to start looking," added Pania.

"And on the last day, after we had crossed a rope bridge and were on the tramping track, we ran right into a rescue team!" said Nikau. "They did what they could for Axel and then offered to carry the stretcher. They radioed for more help. They bandaged up our blisters and gave us snack bars and water. We walked the last mile to the car park beside the road. Then they took us to the hospital. My first ride in an ambulance."

"We were pretty dehydrated and almost had hypothermia, so we had to spend the night there," said Pania.

"That's when you called us," said Ma, smiling.

"Did you tell the rescue team what Axel had done?" asked Stokes.

Nikau and Pania shook their heads.

"We were too tired, relieved… I don't know," said Pania.

"What's Axel's last name?" asked the detective.

"Hexum," said Ma in a whisper.

"Radio that through to Ohakune station," said Stokes to the constable.

They listened to the quick-fire dialogue, between radio static.

"He's held in the hospital for questioning regarding the theft of a vehicle," reported the constable. "He's trying to get out of it by blaming someone called Vito, who had informed on him."

"Right, constable, clear our diaries, we're off to Ohakune. And send this off for fingerprints. We've bagged ourselves a drug dealer."

Nikau felt conflicted. If only Axel had turned from his ways, and started a new life. He wished it didn't have to end this way for his Dad. But he remembered the demented face of an addict. He wanted to help stop this poison from getting onto the streets, and into the hands of young fellas like himself.

"Will you testify against him, lad?" asked the detective.

"Sorry?" He had been daydreaming. The detective repeated the question, laying a heavy hand on his shoulder.

Nikau looked across at Papa Joe, who regarded him with a look of unconditional love, and pride.

"Yes Sir, I will," he said, swallowing down his emotions.

"And so will I," said Pania, standing up and pulling herself straight.

"Thank-you for the bikkies, Miss," said the constable, ducking as he exited the front door.

"You've all been really co-operative. It'll be your word against his, as I suspect we'll find two sets of prints on the meth bag. But your story sounds straight to me, and you have other witnesses, so I reckon you'll be right," said Stokes.

"Sweet," said Nikau, sighing. He hoped Vito would be locked away too. He didn't want anyone turning up looking for him and wanted this whole nightmare to be over.

Nikau heard Joe's rheumy breath behind him as he watched the police car pull off down the street.

"Today, you became a man, son."

He had never heard Papa Joe sounding more sincere, nor solemn.

"Thank you, Pa," he said.

"Now, I'm gonna cook you guys the biggest Samoan feast you've had since Christmas!" he said, rubbing his large hands together. "I'll hire out the church hall and invite everybody. I reckon we need a pig on a spit, some *pani popo, panikeke* and lolly *leis.*"

"But your heart," said Ma.

Papa Joe waved her objection away.

Nikau blinked. "What's the party for Pa?"

"It's a homecoming, son."

Nikau heard a sob and turned around to see Ma, clutching something in her hands. "Oh you fellas!"

Ma stood there, crying. As her tears dropped to the floor, Nikau saw her tension lift. He watched her grey depression evaporate and drift out of the window along with the family secrets. He figured she had wanted him and Pa to get on. And she had been holding her breath that he would turn out okay. That's all. He strode over and bent down to hug her. Pania stood beside them, smiling.

"What you got there, Ma?" he asked?

"Well son, years ago I gave your sister a *pounamu* necklace."

"Yeah, and you didn't give me one."

"I know. I was waiting for the right time." She pushed her soft hands towards him. She unfolded her fingers and placed a paper parcel in his hands. He looked at her. There was an expectation of him. He was ready. He peeled open the paper, casting his eyes on the green *toki* blade. Solid. Stunning. He took a deep breath. Ma took it from him and stretched up to place it around his neck. Nikau lowered his head.

"Courage and strength in times of adversity," she said.

Nikau glanced over at Pania, wondering if she would be envious, but she was smiling with pure joy.

Sometimes, he thought, *you've just got to let love in.*

30

CROSSROADS

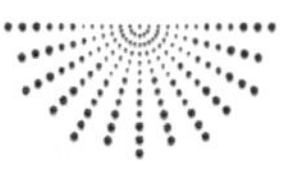

JABU

Jabu sat beneath a woollen sky, watching Kyle surf. Grey light illuminated the landscape in monochrome hues. The steely ocean, iron sand and slate sky toned in as if painted from a limited palette. Jabu felt hollow inside. He tried to explain away his emptiness. *Cloudy day blues*. But that did not allow for him feeling the same yesterday, on a sunny day. Or the day before that.

He watched Kyle carve up a Piha wave, and paddle to shore. The international surf competition was tomorrow. Jabu had been training Kyle hard, every day since they had recovered from the Ruapehu ordeal. He hadn't seen much of Pania, as she was busy with family, but they had spoken on the phone daily.

Kyle wandered up the beach, trying to catch his breath. Jabu threw him a beach towel. Kyle peeled off his wetsuit, dried himself and laid his towel on the dry sand beside Jabu.

"You're looking stylish out there," said Jabu. "And the surf report reckons you'll get six-foot waves tomorrow."

"If this Easterly doesn't ease up, I reckon they're right."

"You've never been daunted by big waves though, eh?"

167

"Nope, six-foot is perfect for me," said Kyle, with confidence.

"Pania tells me she's bringing the whole crew down to Piha tomorrow."

"To watch me?" asked Kyle, looking surprised.

"Yep. Nikau, Ben, Tipene and Areta. They're all coming. They've made a banner." Jabu grinned.

Kyle smiled. "I'd better not let them down then."

"First place?" asked Jabu.

"I'd settle for third," said Kyle, but Jabu knew his friend hoped for better.

"If I place in the top three, I get automatic entry into the tournament in Australia next month."

Jabu nodded.

"You've been a choice training partner. Even though you won the heart of the girl I had my eye on," said Kyle with a wink.

Jabu squirmed.

"It's okay, I'm ribbing you. I told you before, it was no more than a wounded ego. She's too young for me, and it was arrogant of me to expect her to have a crush just because I did."

"Well no, that wasn't arrogant…" said Jabu.

"Anyway, you two suit each other," said Kyle. Jabu noticed that the twisted expression of jealousy had lifted from his friend's face. Kyle seemed relaxed, and genuine.

Jabu stared out to sea.

"But, girls aside, I want to ask if you'll come to Aussie with me bro?"

Jabu didn't hesitate. "I can't, sorry."

"Why not?"

"I promised Alexia I'd be back in time to support her at the Junior South African champs," he said. "And my air ticket is booked."

"I get it, and there's Green Room House."

Those three words stirred something in Jabu. A recognition of the hollow place in his abdomen. He had a home shaped hole, sitting in the centre of his solar plexus. The landscape of New Zealand was dazzling, yet he missed the rugged landscape of his roots. He got thinking about Green Room House in soundbites and flashes of a face, a familiar smell — a feeling. He heard the expressive chattering of voices in his mother language. Zulu. He missed the taste of it on his tongue. The way it was not considered rude to shout out hello to someone across the street. He heard a tinkling of laughter. He thought about how wonderful it felt when a new child came to the house and laughed for the first time. Green Room House. He could smell boerewors cooked on a *braai* and taste the sweet tanginess of Mrs Balls Chutney. He pictured his friends — but they were more than friends — they were his family.

"Yes, Green Room House," said Jabu. "I'm homesick." There, he had said it.

"I understand. But what about Pania?"

Jabu had never met anyone like her and doubted he ever would again. He didn't want to leave her and didn't think it fair to ask her to join him. All her family were here. On Pania's daily phone calls, she had told him how Nikau and Papa Joe were building something new. How delighted she was to be around them, as they laughed and cherished one another. He couldn't ask her to leave her whanau.

Jabu shrugged. He had no answers.

"What if she asks you to stay?" asked Kyle.

"She hasn't."

"But she might. She's been busy with family stuff, and you've been surfing every spare minute. What do you reckon you would do if she asked you?"

"I don't know," said Jabu, looking down at his numb toes.

"Ah bro," said Kyle, giving his arm a friendly nudge. "I can see you're burdened. Don't worry, there are many fish in the sea."

Jabu looked at the sea and thought about the idiom. He didn't agree with it at all. Girls were more like pearls than fish. Pania was a rare find, and their meeting was so serendipitous. But, he didn't think he could give up his home, even for a pearl. In his nostalgia, he forgot how restless he had been feeling in his daily routine at Green Room House. He remembered only what he missed.

"Hey, cheer up bro. Look, I'm gonna buy us each a burger and one of those long giraffe milkshakes."

"Chur," said Jabu, grinning.

"You've picked up the lingo," said Kyle.

They both laughed and wandered up the beach to the local cafe.

The next day, Kyle performed at his peak and took away first place at the tournament. Jabu was thrilled. It was an honour to have been his training partner, and Jabu felt a personal fulfilment in Kyle's success. They had been surfing side by side for many years. Jabu had seen Kyle surf with epic style in the past, but today was absolute perfection.

After the interviews and formalities were over, Kyle offered to shout the jubilant group of friends lunch at an upmarket cafe in Piha.

Jabu sat quietly observing the group, taking in the moment. Nikau seemed starstruck by Kyle's celebrity status and asked him to sign his t-shirt. Kyle laughed humbly as he signed it, and said, "I can do better than that, I'll give you some surfing lessons before I go." Ben and Tipene sat up straight at the table and remembered their manners with the waitress. Areta and Pania chatted about everything and anything. Pania sat beside Jabu, her hand in his under the table, perhaps to be discrete.

Jabu thought about his role going forward in Kyle's career. He figured he had helped Kyle as much as he was able, and that from now on, Kyle would need a professional coach.

"Hey bro, I've been thinking," he blurted out across the table. "The competition is going to get tougher as you get to the next level and I reckon you'll need a pro coach going forward. And since I can't come with you, I suggest you seriously think about that eh?"

Kyle looked across the table at him earnestly. "You're right, yes. But let's not think about that now. It's time to celebrate what we've achieved together. Let's raise a toast to Jabu!" said Kyle.

Glasses were raised and clinked together. Out of respect for Ben and Tipene who were doing well in their rehabilitation, they only drank soft drinks, coffee or hot chocolates. Jabu noticed that Kyle had kept his victory bottle of bubbly under the table for another occasion.

"Thank you, Jabu for your convention-breaking input over the years," Kyle added. "I couldn't have got here without you!"

"Cheers!" they roared and everyone clapped or whooped.

Jabu waved for them to stop, half enjoying it.

"You could be a coach yourself, you know," said Kyle directly.

"Well, I am. I coach the children," said Jabu, folding his arms.

"I know. But I think someone up-and-coming could benefit from your experience. I can think of a few rising stars at Green Room House for a start..."

Jabu shrugged and glanced over at Pania. Her effervescent expression quickly changed. He thought her eyes spoke of sadness at the idea of him having another life, far away. He squeezed her hand and took a giant bite of pizza so that he couldn't be expected to say anything.

The next morning Kyle swung the motel door open and greeted Jabu with a goofy grin. He handed over a takeaway burger and chips, and an envelope.

"You've got mail, dude. It's from Green Room House. Go on, open it!"

Jabu tore open the envelope and read it while biting into a juicy burger. Mayonnaise dribbled down his chin. *It sure beats possum stew, he thought.*

"It's from Alexia," he said to Kyle while chewing.

Alexia

    Durban, South Africa

Hi Jabu,

    I hope you and Kyle are enjoying yourselves in New Zealand. Please wish Kyle good luck for the surf competition. Tell him to go hard out!

She must have written this before the comp. She'll be stoked to hear Kyle won, thought Jabu. He continued reading.

I only got third place in the last local comp. I was so disappointed. I've been training with Billie, but to be honest, she doesn't push me hard enough.

    I need your help Jabu! I hope you get back in time to help me get up to scratch for the Junior SA champs. We always used to train so well together. Nobody pushes me to get outrageous aerials like you do.

    By the way, I do have some good news to share. My sponsor has said that they will pay for me to have a professional coach in the future! I've placed an advert in the local 'Splash!' magazine. Hopefully, I'll find someone who is just right.

    Anyway, enough about me. The kids are missing you (and Kyle) so much. Billie, Philemon, Josh and Vusi do a pretty good job of running things. But sometimes I hear some of the younger kids crying themselves to sleep. You're like their teenage Dad. They love you and look up to you, and well, Green Room House is not the same without you. It's hard.

    Well, that's all from me. Hope to see you soon.

    Your buddy

Alexia (aka 'Gecko') - Don't even go there!

Jabu finished reading, then folded the letter. "They're missing us, dude," he said to Kyle, passing his friend the letter to read.

He would reply tomorrow. He needed time to think.

A day later, Jabu penned his reply. He licked the envelope and sealed it. Then he pulled up his hoodie and walked down the street to the post shop. He stood at the red post box, his hand holding the envelope above the slot, suspended in mid-air. An image of Pania flashed before his eyes. They were standing in the forest. She had a ski hood pulled over her silky black hair. Her almond-shaped eyes gazed at him, and her mouth turned up at the corners in a shy smile.

His hand hovered at the envelope slot. He pulled the letter back an inch, clutching it tight.

Then he imagined the children at Green Room House, singing him a welcome song. He sighed, posted the letter, and walked away.

3 1

AN EPHEMERAL MOMENT

PANIA

There was not a breath of wind this peachy October day, and the unbroken waves rolled in like smooth tin foil. Pania felt like she needed to pay attention to the moment. There was not an aspect of it that she would change to make it more perfect, besides making it last. But nothing lasts forever. Perfect moments are as flighty as butterflies, alighting with bright-winged brilliance and perishing soon after. Pania knew she needed to focus on this moment and try to cherish it. To be fully present. Things change, and then all one has is the regret of not having vividly been there, in the now.

She looked across at Jabu, who sat on his surfboard beside her, bobbing up and down on the swell. His braided hair pulled back with a hair-tie, made way for an intelligent forehead. His dark skin glistened with saltwater. He must have felt her gaze, as he turned, and flashed her a smile. Was there sadness in his smile? Something he needed to tell her?

Jabu and Kyle had spent a few days training up Nikau after the surf competition. Today her brother had gained enough confidence to paddle out to the backline for the first time. He chatted to Kyle;

174

relaxed, laughing together. She marvelled at how Nikau had gained in spirit and self-belief. Not long ago, he was monosyllabic. All shrugs and grunts, but now he was sharing a joke and chatting with this pro surfer as if they were old friends.

There is something about being in a pressure situation that will either bind you or turn you into lifelong foes. Pania felt that the Ruapehu ordeal had bound the four of them, making them unusually close. Fellow survivors.

A wave loomed up, and Panic watched as Kyle encouraged Nikau to catch it. It was larger than any he had caught before, but he paddled hard. With the nimbleness of a natural snowboarder, her brother jumped to his feet and balanced down the face of the wave, carving at the bottom, but falling as he tried to cut back at the lip.

They all cheered. Pania realised that for the first time in ages, she felt contented. Her bro had stopped drinking and smoking weed. He had given up the party scene and was well stoked on surfing, snow-boarding, and anything outdoorsy. Better still, he had developed leadership qualities and had begun to help her fundraise for surfboards. Nikau had told Pania that he wanted to get all his mates into surfing.

She may not have succeeded in her quest to get him to snowboard down the glacier, but on that mountain, Nikau had changed. He had looked into the eyes of someone broken. Not wanting the face of an addict to become the face in the mirror, her brother had rejected that life. A weight lifted off her shoulders as she watched him laugh and play in the surf; free.

After a while, Pania's arms felt heavy.

"Jabu, I'm gonna catch a wave in," she said. "I'm puffed."

"I'll join you," he said, paddling after her.

They caught a sweet ride, laughing as they surfed the wave together.

"Nikau and Kyle will carry on for a while," she said, flicking her wet hair over her shoulder as they walked up the beach.

"Can I buy you a coffee or ice cream?" asked Jabu, unzipping his wetsuit and rolling it down to his waist. He wrapped a towel around his shoulders.

"A coffee would be nice, thanks. You cold?"

"Hehe, yes. It's my African blood. I'm used to the Indian ocean," he said.

"Fair enough," said Pania.

They walked over to the beachfront cafe, where Jabu paid for coffees. Their feet dangled as they perched on the car park wall, facing the ocean. They were silent for a while as if summoning the courage to approach the topic of their imminent parting.

Jabu spoke first. "Do you remember what day tomorrow is?" He cleared his throat.

"Oh heck, is it your departure flight?" It had crept up on her.

"Yes, it is. We're going to have to say goodbye today."

"Oh. I see," said Pania. She fiddled with her pounamu necklace. "Unless… unless you decide to stay, you know, for personal reasons," she said. Pania did not want to spell it out. She hoped he would stay for her.

Jabu didn't answer, his brown eyes almost slate in a moody reflection of the sea.

"I was wondering if you'll be my Tongariro?" she asked. It had felt as if she was Pirongia, and Jabu and Kyle were sparring for her. But Jabu's expression gave her a sinking feeling.

"I, I can't stay, Pania. Africa is my home," he began. "I have responsibilities…"

That perfect moment… how many days do butterflies live? Had the moment already started to unravel?

"It's not supposed to be like this," she objected. "In the myth of Ruapehu, you're supposed to beat your rival, Kyle, and then stay. He leaves, and we stay together… Pirongia and Tongariro…" She was babbling, and she knew it.

Jabu pursed his lips. He stared out at the ocean as if searching for words.

"Maybe we can look at it another way," he said finally. "The true heart of your story is this… it's a story about whanau, and loyalty, in this case. Let's say, you're Pirongia, and your brother Nikau is Tongariro. He ended up defeating Axel, who is Taranaki, to save you. Axel will not be allowed near either of you. But deep down, Nikau cries for him. For the father that he was supposed to be. These tears form the river, Whanganui that runs from Nikau to Axel, forming a deep valley."

"And who is Ruapehu?" asked Pania.

"That's your Papa Joe, always watching over the two of you."

Pania was crying inside. Moved by the poignant truth of the story. A young man, sensitive enough to perceive it that way, was the very young man who was trying to break it to her that he was leaving. Still, she cared too much for him to make him suffer for his choice. She rallied and smiled bravely.

"I like that version," she said.

Jabu shuffled over and swung his arm around her. She rested her head on his broad shoulder.

"Nikau is doing so well now. He's getting good marks at school. He's clean. And he is well into helping me with AOA. He's taken Tipene and Ben under his wing, and others are wanting to sign up to our next adventure. He's even started coming to church with us on Sundays."

Jabu's warm smile reminded Pania of the African savanna. How she wanted to beg him to stay. Or to follow him to Africa. But then she saw Nikau coming out of the water grinning, followed by Kyle, who whooped and cheered at her brother's epic wave.

"I, I couldn't be happier really," said Pania, before the dam wall broke and the tears began to flow.

"Alexia and the other kids need me Pania. I'm their family, you see…"

"Shh, you don't need to explain," she said. She couldn't follow him. Her whanau was whole now, and this is where she needed to be. Somehow she had to say goodbye to this handsome Zulu surfer, who had stolen her heart.

Pania leaned across and kissed him softly. He wrapped her in an embrace and held her in his strong arms. She could feel his heart beating. Steady, like an African drum.

"*Ka kite anō*," he said. He had learnt a few words in her language.

"*Hamba kahle*," she whispered in Zulu, looking up at his big brown eyes and repeating the words he had taught her. "Shall I come to the airport?"

"No, that will be too sad," said Jabu. "I'll visit New Zealand again someday."

"What if I'm taken by then?" asked Pania.

"I expect you will be," said Jabu sadly. "I can't expect you to…"

"I understand," she said, putting her finger on his lips. "Whanau. Katiakitanga. Home. I totally get it."

"You've always got me," he said, his eyebrows raising in the centre of his forehead.

The perfect moment was over. A butterfly lay beneath the foot of a toddler, both wings crumpled. Unable to take flight.

"I'll never forget our adventure," said Jabu, "and your strong, beautiful heart."

Nikau and Kyle wandered up from the beach. Pania switched gears.

"Nikau, say goodbye to your mates, we need to get going," she said, throwing him the car keys.

"Am I driving?" he asked.

"Yep, you've got your learner's."

"Your car, sis?"

"Yep, sure. Now say goodbye to these fellas. They fly tomorrow."

"You're kidding, right?"

Jabu and Kyle shook their heads.

"I'm off to Australia for another competition," said Kyle, "and Jabu is heading back to South Africa."

Nikau nodded slowly, his smile fading.

"Cheers for saving us from your wicked Dad," said Jabu, only half-joking. Nikau shook Jabu's hand firmly and leaned in for a hug, patting him on the back. Kyle and Nikau did the same. Then Kyle hugged Pania briefly.

"Thanks for everything," Kyle said to his hosts. "It's been unforgettable."

Jabu held Pania for the last time. Then she toughened herself up, flicked her hair over her shoulder and turned to go.

"C'mon Nikau, before I change my mind about you driving," she said, striding towards the car, and not turning back.

32

A SURPRISE

JABU

Two months after the eruption, Jabu stood at the shoreline of the Indian ocean and gazed at the Southern Cross, comforted that Pania could see this star formation. At least they were in the same hemisphere. That was something.

The prosecutor had won his case. Axel had been locked up and had a strict trespassing order against him. The man would not come near his children again. Jabu and Pania had exchanged a letter each, something they would continue to do for a while. But now that Jabu was here, and she there, their connection seemed tenuous, like the thread of a spiderweb.

Yet he only had to remember that night in the forest when the mountain was erupting, and a veil of ash sifted down, and the moonlight came and went behind a cloud, and something inside him ached. He remembered her face, as the silver light illuminated it, looking up at him. They were anxious and afraid but comforted by their growing closeness. She was his first kiss.

His memory of her intertwined with vivid images of Aotearoa. It blended with distinct scents, like peppery kawakawa tea, and sounds,

180

like the swooshing flight of a kererū. Fear and relief mingled as he remembered the wall of snow sliding down the slope towards them, and then recalled her bravery. When he thought of Pania, he imagined her almond eyes and green pounamu necklace, the call of a ruru in a kauri tree, the sound of her laughter, the stories of her people. He looked up at the crescent moon. Would she see it at a different angle? He laughed aloud at his silliness.

Then Jabu picked up his surfboard. It was too dark to risk a surf. He had come down to the beach to catch a quick wave but had found himself lost in memories, admiring the stars in their shared sky.

Pania, he thought, savouring her name. He sighed and began the two-block walk back to Green Room House.

Lights were on in the double story townhouse. Home. He opened the green front door, still lost in a reverie. The house smelled of barbecue sauce and chocolate. He walked down the passage into the dining room.

"Surprise!" they all yelled at once.

A banner hung along the back wall. "Happy Birthday!" it read in bright gold lettering.

A gathering of children, and friends, all beamed at him. Billie was there; the girl he once believed to be a mermaid — who had rescued him the day he tried to surf before he could swim. A child clutched her left hand, and an infant clung to her right leg. Vusi and Sipho, the street children who had taken him to their shelter when he had no coins to call his Auntie, stood side by side. They were still the best of friends. Philemon and Thabo, the leaders of "Father's boys" street gang, both had strong roles at Green Room House. They had never looked back. And Teacher-Josh was there. Was he visiting especially for the party?

A feast covered every inch of the table. Jabu's eyes scanned the spread hungrily. There were plates piled high with barbecued chicken wings, drumsticks and cocktail sausages. Quiches, hot sausage rolls and freshly baked chocolate brownies emitted mouthwatering aromas. Sneaky children's fingers reached up to snaffle a morsel. But that's not all. There were crisps and dips, veggie sticks, cheese and crackers, Billie's *melktert* and a bowl of caramel popcorn.

"Aw guys," he said, smiling at them all, "this is awesome!" He scanned the familiar faces. But he wondered why Alexia, the surf prodigy wasn't there.

"There's more," said Billie, turning to the doorway that led from the kitchen. Alexia wheeled Ice through the door. His old friend! The one who had lured him into 'surfing' on a train, the one who had lost the use of his legs, but found himself by caring for baby rhinos. Ice flashed a mouth of pearly white teeth in a broad grin. He carried an enormous cake on his lap. It looked as if it had been iced by the children. Twenty candles burned brightly, dripping their wax on the frosting. Alexia started the Happy Birthday song. The excited fidget of children and Jabu's loyal friends all joined her in a hearty rendition.

Jabu took the cake from Ice's lap and placed it on the table. Before blowing out the candles, he turned to give his friend a Sowetan handshake.

"Blow out the candles," shouted the youngest child.

Jabu blew with all his lung capacity, but one candle remained lit.

"Aah, you've got a girlfriend!" teased Ice. Jabu smiled knowingly and gently blew out the last candle.

3 3

NEW BEGINNINGS

JABU

Jabu woke before sunrise. He felt restless. Not even the epic New Zealand adventure had wiped out the feeling. He had only been back in the old routine for two weeks, and the scratchiness had begun to rise again. It was like the teeth of a dog, gnawing on a bone. He couldn't shake it. He rubbed the sleep from his eyes, pulled on his board-shorts and crept out the house, down the passage, past the dreaming children. He loved those children, and the teens too.

Jabu closed the heavy front door, locked it, and walked barefoot across the dew-drenched lawn. As the tin door of the surf shed creaked open, he remembered another tin door, closing for the last time. It was the door to the shack he had lived in with his Mama before she died. It was a memory he pushed under, most times. But in the still of predawn, all alone in the quiet darkness of the yard, he let the memory surface.

He had slept in the shack, on his own that night. It was a night of dark terrors. When a rooster woke the village before first light, he had made up his mind that he would leave the lonely hut. He would never sleep on his own again if he could help it. He would make his way to Durban and find his Auntie.

Jabu shuddered. It was cold in the garden before sunrise. He pulled out his waxy surfboard and shut the tin door. It was unlike the door of the shack, which had no hinges. Merely a rectangle of tin that he slid in front of the space, and wedged down with a brick. He had stood there, all of twelve years old, outside the threshold of the only home he had ever known, and took a strident step forward. He hadn't thought that he would never go back. He only knew he had to keep moving forward.

Presently he walked down the road to the beach. The sea called to him as it had the first morning he had woken up in Durban. As he walked, he thought about the friends he had made. Sipho and Vusi and 'Father's' lost boys. He thought about Billie, who had taught him to surf, and Kyle. Gallons of water had passed under the bridge of their friendship! He remembered Auntie, and his cousins, and how he had felt as loved as a sharp stone in a shoe. He wasn't sure which was lonelier — being on his own in the tin shack, or living at Auntie's. But the shack was scarier.

He wondered if that night had caused some deep scarring. The night he had lain in bed thinking about his Mama, and smelling her hair oil as he sobbed on her mattress. He'd had visions of Ice's body, carried away on a stretcher after the trainsurfing accident. He thought about the Tokoloshe and how the bed was raised on bricks and how he had prayed all through the night.

Green Room House was the answer to prayer. He had prayed for a home, and he had asked God for a new family. Auntie and his cousins had not felt like home, but Green Room House did. From the first day, people he cared about surrounded him. Billie and Kyle, Philemon and Thabo, and then Vusi and Sipho. Soon there were more children — Bongani, and Alexia, the little pro surfers. Compared to the desolation he had felt, this was rich.

So why did he feel agitated now? He welcomed the soft sand beneath his toes after walking on the tarmac. Even the familiar sound of the Indian Ocean waves failed to soothe him. The sky turned to indigo, and the morning star flickered. Jabu sat on the moist sand near the tide line. He attached his surf leash to his ankle. Was it only Pania he longed for?

No, he decided it was something else. Like an undiscovered destiny. A purpose that he should be stretching towards. Pania had shown him a possibility. That he could love and be loved, know and be known. One day he might want to marry someone, and have children. But his salary at Green Room House was modest. Sure he had board and lodging, and a job that he used to cherish, but... Oh, he didn't know! Thinking about it was annoying. He needed to wait a few more minutes until the sun had risen, and then he could surf and try to forget his angst. He'd become more nervous about sharks lately, and did not want to offer them breakfast by surfing at dawn.

Jabu was so lost in his tumultuous thoughts that he didn't hear Alexia approaching. She sat down beside him, plonking her surfboard on the sand. Jabu startled.

"Gosh, you're jumpy," Alexia said, examining his face. "You okay? You're looking stressed out."

Jabu thought about whether he could put his feelings into words. Alexia was a good friend, and he needed to offload. He decided to try.

"I guess I'm feeling frustrated. Remember how I gave up an opportunity to attend a surf academy, so I could stay on at Green Room House?"

"Yes, many years ago," she said. "That was noble."

"Well, I didn't see it as being noble. I needed to be here, as much as the children needed me."

"But...?"

"But, now, I feel as if I've allowed myself to be too comfortable. Doing the same thing, day in, and day out. I'm like a snake needing to shed skin. I need a new challenge. I need a career opportunity. It's time for me to grow up, Gecko."

Alexia glared at him. "Quit calling me that."

"Sorry, Lexie," he said. Usually, her reaction gave him a broad grin, but today, he felt incapable of even a smile.

"What if that opportunity was my one and only chance, at being somebody?"

"You are somebody — to all of us," she countered.

"I know, but I never did become a competitive surfer. I gave that up for a place called home, and for a chance to rescue the boys. What if that's all I ever do?"

Alexia had begun to smile. Jabu thought that was an insensitive response. She was nodding now and beaming, her white pearlies greeting the dawn. Then she laughed, her braids bobbing up and down.

"It's not funny," Jabu said sulkily.

"Why didn't I think of it before?" said Alexia, shaking her head.

"Think of what?"

"You, as a coach."

"What?"

"You could be my coach."

"What are you going on about? I've always coached you, but now you can afford a professional coach."

"What if I said to you that you're the best coach I could ever have? I want you to be my professional coach. I've checked out all the job applicants, and none of them sounds half as inspiring as you are," she said, looking shyly at her pink painted toenails.

Jabu could hardly believe what he was hearing.

"What if everything you've done at Green Room House — training me and bringing me success — helping the kids, learning from Kyle ... what if it has made you who you are today? A mature young man who brings out the best in me, and is ready to be my professional coach?"

Jabu stared at Alexia, trying to ascertain if there was any inkling of teasing in her expression.

"I've never been more sincere," she said as if reading his mind.

Jabu gulped. His heart had begun to race, and he wanted to jump up and fist pump the sky. But then he remembered the children. Peter Pan's lost boys. He was their captain.

"How can I abandon the children?"

"You won't be — we can stay at the house, and train here. You may not be with them as often as before, and sometimes we'll travel. But it won't be a clean break — more like a weaning period."

"Who'll…" Jabu stopped himself before his voice broke. He would not let Alexia see his tenderness. He cleared his throat and watched a seagull soaring inches above the waves. When he felt ready, he tried again. "Who will be their captain?" he asked.

"Their captain? Jabu, that Peter Pan book really got to you."

"I mean, I dunno, their father figure?"

"Well, unless you haven't noticed; Philemon, Thabo and Vusi all do an excellent job with the children. They're always vying with each other for more leadership opportunities. How about you step aside and let them?"

This was it. The destiny Jabu had been itching to stretch into. The future had been tugging at him like an outgoing tide, unsettling his comfort zone.

"Oh boy, that's a clean break," said Alexia, eyeing the surf.

The sky blushed with morning colour, the air smelled salty, and Jabu's skin tingled. *Thank you, Lord*, he thought.

"When do I start?" he asked. He smiled at her in thanks.

Alexia leapt to her feet, picking up her surfboard. "Now!" she said. "Race you in!"

After a vigorous training session, Jabu and Alexia rested on their boards, beyond the breakers where the swells rolled in beneath them. Alexia talked excitedly about her goals, her dreams, and the upcoming tournaments on her schedule.

"You'll still get to be here for the kids whenever we're at home, but you will need to travel with me when I have an international comp," said Alexia.

Jabu nodded.

"The children will be fine. They have a whole team of strong leaders around them. And they'll get to see you often, no?"

"You're right," said Jabu, beginning to realise that he was not the only positive role model for the children. Green Room House was a family, and he was one member. No longer the filament that held them together. He was free to grow, to travel and to support Alexia.

"So, where are we headed then?" he asked.

"Well, first up there's a comp in the USA, then Hawaii, and then, later on, we'll go to New Zealand and Australia. I can't wait to see the world!"

New Zealand. The words were heavy with meaning. Aotearoa, the land of the long white cloud. Pania's home. How could he travel to New Zealand without visiting Pania? But how could he expect her to see him after he had left her? What if she had moved on, and met someone else? She might refuse to see him. To be in that beautiful land, without seeing the fairness of her face, or hearing her lyrical voice would be a type of mourning.

Jabu pictured the rugged Piha beach. He imagined himself not on a roller in the Indian Ocean, facing East, but sitting out the backline of the Tasman Sea, facing West. The sentinels rose grandly, framing the bay, and in his imagination, he embedded himself into the dramatic setting. He couldn't but picture Pania, happening to rise up into view, paddling hard to make it over a cresting wave. She flicked her black hair over her shoulders, and realising she was beyond the break line, looked across — at him. Her eyes met his and instantly registered the betrayal. That he had come to New Zealand and had not called on her. He remembered that expression from the night she believed Nikau had played turncoat in the cave. *Oh, Pania.*

Jabu couldn't let their story unfold that way. He would write to her, hoping there was space in her heart to see him again — with no promises, no solution to their distance — but with the same deep need to reconnect. If she refused to meet him, he resolved, at least he would know that he had reached out.

"Gosh coach, you're quiet," said Alexia sulkily.

"Sorry Lexie, it's just … I have a …" he paused, trying to find the right words. "I have a friend in New Zealand. I was wondering whether she will want to see me again, is all."

"A female friend! Is she a girlfriend?" asked Alexia, brightening at the idea of a romantic story.

"I don't really know," said Jabu, watching as a seagull landed on the water.

Alexia opened her mouth to blurt out a flurry of questions but stopped herself. Jabu realised his expression, at once dreamy and anguished, earnest and secretive, must have signalled to Alexia that this was his own private dilemma.

After the surf, Jabu and Alexia walked the two blocks back to Green Room House.

"Bags a shower," said Alexia, skipping off ahead of him.

Jabu stopped out of habit at the post box. He lifted the green lid and collected a pile of bills and flyers. He flicked through them unconsciously, when something caught his eye. An aerogramme. On the stamp, a thumbnail photograph caught his attention. In it, Mount Ruapehu and Tongariro loomed in their white robes over Lake Taupō.

Standing outside the yard, in his board shorts, Jabu placed his surfboard down, and carefully tore the letter open:

Hi Jabu,

I miss you. I cried into my pillow last night. You feel so far away.

Don't get me wrong, I'm fine. Happy even. Nikau is a mentor to a bunch of at-risk kids, and I am so proud of him. Aotearoa Ora Adventures is going strong. We have another trip to Ruapehu planned, and we may even ski that glacier. This time Nikau has agreed to go on skis, so he doesn't fall behind!

But I think of you often, and miss your smile. I think of our kiss and hold it as my most cherished memory. If I could spend half an hour with you, to talk, to laugh, to remember our story, then maybe I could let go. Even if it meant another tearful goodbye — I might be able to cope better. I might be able to move on.

Please know that you are welcome here. If you ever visit Aotearoa, please look me up. Even if you're married, or old — if you care to see me — do! And if you aren't old or married, and get here soon — and if you still feel half as much for me as I do for you, well who knows what the future may have in store for us.

Boldly and sincerely

Arohanui

Pania

Jabu smiled to himself. A warm glow radiated from his core outwards, to his fingers and toes. The future spread out before him. A vast landscape of country roads, leading here or there. Each left or right fork, a choice, leading to further crossroads, y-bends, twists and turns. The future is an ocean — at once a hue, then a shimmer and a different tone or shade. As you try to name it — blue, green, turquoise, silver or grey, it morphs into something different. Turn your back on the swells, and they rise into dumpers. Or the wind drops and you sit for hours, waiting for the excitement of the faintest ripple.

Attempting to write their story, his, and Pania's, to premeditate or guess at what might unfold, would serve no purpose but frustrate him. But stepping bravely into the landscape with a multitude of roads spreading out like capillaries; or diving into an ocean that refuses to conform to a single colour or temperament, trusting God on the journey — that was the mutable substance of life.

The end

BIBLIOGRAPHY

Department of Conservation and Tongariro Natural History Society. 1998. *The Restless Land. Stories of Tongariro National Park World Heritage Area.* Everbest Printing Co., Ltd. 156p.

Gregg, D.R. 1961. *Volcanoes of Tongariro National Park.* New Zealand Geological Survey Handbook, Information Series No. 28. New Zealand Department of Scientific and Industrial Research. 82p.

Williams, K. & Keys, H. 2008. *Ruapehu Erupts.* Fully Updated Edition. Random House New Zealand. 64p.

ACKNOWLEDGMENTS

AND AUTHOR'S NOTES

This story is a song in praise of this land, Aotearoa and its people. The *tangata whenua* and the *tangata tiriti* have shown our family immense kindness and generosity. My gratitude abounds to the people of this country, for accepting us as Kiwi citizens and giving us a new home.

On one of our first ski trips to Mount Ruapehu, we stopped at the visitor centre and stood in front of the statue of Te Heuheu Tukino Horonuku. We read that he had gifted the peaks to the Crown in 1887, after gaining the approval of the Tūwharetoa tribes. Decades later, Tongariro National Park became a World Heritage Site. With its volcanic activity, and rich Māori legends and stories, the centre of the north island captured my imagination. This book pays tribute to the people of Tūwharetoa and this captivating place.

I also want to acknowledge the excellent ski field operation of Mt Ruapehu, run at Whakapapa and Tūroa. Our family has enjoyed five seasons skiing and snowboarding on these well maintained ski fields.

While I have written about a real historical event (the eruptions of September 1995) at a real place, the story is entirely a work of fiction.

I want to thank Nick, Emma and Dylan, for encouraging me on my writing journey. Without you, my loves, I would not be grounded enough to write. You are my world.

Thank you Nick, my Geologist husband for your expertise on all things relating to Earth Science.

Thank you to my beta readers for your input - especially Kate Darbishire (author of 'Speechless'), Eve & Ant, Nick, Adam, Micah & Fiona and Michelle. Your input helped me to improve the story and I so appreciate your time and honest communication.

I also want to share that Nikau's story is essentially a prodigal one and springs from my Christian faith.

"'For this son of mine was dead and is alive again; he was lost and is found.' So they began to celebrate." Luke 15:24 (NIV)

Jabu's story is the conclusion of the trilogy that began with 'Trainsurfer', where a young homeless boy struggles to find a place called home, and ends with him striding out into his future.

If you started by reading Nikau's Escape and would like to read 'Trainsurfer' and 'Saving Thandi', please visit my website. Perhaps the threads will weave together and enhance your experience.

ABOUT THE AUTHOR

Kate S Richards lives in New Zealand with her husband and two teenage children, as well as two dogs, two cats and two guinea pigs. She works as a school librarian. Kate grew up in South Africa.

The Adventures of Jabu & Friends

Book 1: Trainsurfer
Book 2: Saving Thandi
Book 3: Nikau's Escape
These books can be read as stand alone adventures.

If you would like a free EBook of Trainsurfer, please visit KateSRichards.com and sign up to the readers group.

Trainsurfer - Book 1

An orphan, running from loss, trying to survive in an oppressive regime. Drawn to the lure of the ocean. A chance find — a broken surfboard on a beach promises something new.

Can Jabu find a place to call home? Is there a way he can help the homeless "Father's boys"? Is forgiveness possible?

Saving Thandi - Book 2

After an accident that left Ice with a permanent disability, the last thing he needs is an adventure.

The trouble is, the rhinos need saving, his friends are in danger, and he may be the caring hero they all need.